# in the box called pleasure

stories by kim addonizio

**FC2**

Normal/Tallahassee

Published by FC2 with support provided by Florida
State University, the Unit for Contemporary Litera-
ture of the Department of English at Illinois State
University, and the Illinois Arts Council


Address all inquiries to: Fiction Collective Two, Florida
State University, c/o English Department, Tallahassee, FL
32306-1580

ISBN: Paper, 1-57366-081-7

**Library of Congress Cataloging-in-Publication Data**
Addonizio, Kim
In the box called pleasure: stories/by Kim Addonizio --
1st ed.
p. cm.
ISBN 1-57366-081-7 (alk. paper)
1. United States--Social life and customs--20th century--
Fiction. I. Title.
PS3551.D3997 I5 1999
813'.54--dc21                                        99-045089
                                                         CIP


Cover Design: Todd Michael Bushman
Book Design: Owen Thomas Williams

Produced and printed in the United States of America
Printed on recycled paper with soy ink

Illinois **ARTS** Council
AN AGENCY OF
THE STATE OF ILLINOIS

This program is partially sponsored by a grant from the Illinois Arts Council

*for aya*

# acknowledgments

My deepest thanks to Jay Schaefer, who encouraged my very earliest efforts at fiction. Thanks also to Mark Pritchard, editor of *Frighten the Horses*. I'm grateful to the writers who read the manuscript, in whole or in part, and offered editorial advice: Mimi Albert, Robin Beeman, Janice Eidus, Toni Graham, and Lori Wood. And to Cris Mazza, for asking.

Thanks to the editors of the following publications where these stories previously appeared, some in slightly different form: "Trip" in *Caprice*; "But" and "Flash Suppressor" in *Chelsea*; "Inside Out" in *Five Fingers Review*; "Bedtime Story" in *Frighten the Horses*; "Reading Sontag" in *Gargoyle*; "The Chair" and "Survivors" in *Gettysburg Review*; "Testimony" in *Montserrat Review*; "Gas" in *Santa Clara Review*.

"In The Box Called Pleasure" appeared in an anthology, *Breaking Up Is Hard To Do*, from the Crossing Press; "Reading" appeared in *Chick Lit: Postfeminist Fiction*, published by FC2; "The Gift" appeared in *Dick for a Day* from Villard Books; "A Brief History of Condoms" appeared in *Getting It On: A Condom Reader* from Soho Press and also in *Libido* on the Web; "Inside Out" also appeared in *Hard Love: Writings on Intimacy and Violence* from Queen of Swords Press; "Til There Was You" was included in *It's Only Rock and Roll: Rock and Roll Short Stories* from David Godine; "Survivors" also appeared in *Microfictions* from W.W. Norton and in *The Norton Book of Love*.

Note: "Reading Sontag" is indebted to, and borrows lines from, Susan Sontag's essay "The Pornographic Imagination."

# contents

# the fall of saigon

When Dennis met Angel she was pregnant and seeing two men, only one of whom knew about the other. There was no question which one was the father; it had happened, she was sure, that night in the tiny booth at the topless place where, for a quarter, you could have privacy and three minutes of flipping channels from orgies to masturbation to scenes with whips and leather and complicated equipment. You could hear what channel was playing in the next booth, so it really wasn't all that private. They'd had to be quiet, especially in the in-between seconds when the time ran out on the loops and they had to stop and put more money in.

But now all that was over. A couple of hours after seeing Dennis walk into the bar where she worked, serving him shots of schnapps and watching how his left hand

11

occasionally, unconsciously, moved to stroke his chest, at last call Angel had scrawled her address and phone number across the front of his white T-shirt. The next morning she made two short phone calls to tie up the loose ends, and Dennis put his scuffed black combat boots next to her spike-heeled thigh-high leather ones, and the two of them proceeded to drink and fuck their way through the rest of the week.

Meanwhile she was throwing up in the mornings.

"It's cool," Dennis said. He loved her ass. He loved the black tattooed thorns that circled her waist. When he put his hands there, he thought he could feel them, pricking him slightly. He was twenty-four and had never been in love. Before meeting Angel, he'd been bored out of his mind. Being with Angel was better than any drugs he'd taken so far.

"I have to go to the clinic," Angel said.

"No problem," Dennis said.

"I can't have a goddamned baby." She was crying. He loved how she cried. He loved wiping her face after she threw up, as he was doing now. She crawled into his arms in her bathroom, and he stroked her red hair. Angel's bathroom was filthy. There were brownish rings around the sink and inside the toilet bowl.

Angel made little whimpering sounds as she cried, and rubbed her eyes with her fists.

"I'm so fucked up," Angel moaned.

Dennis took one of her hands in his and marveled at it—plump and white and sweet as cookie dough, with daggerlike nails painted metallic green. He loved her brown roots, her smeary black eye makeup. He rocked her in his pale, skinny arms and thought, I am your man.


They had to stop twice on the way to the clinic, so Angel could get out of Dennis's old Chevy and kneel by the side of the highway, gagging and sweating. When they got there they still had some time to kill, so they went to a bar and had a few beers. The bar had doll parts hanging from the ceiling—heads, arms, legs—along with bicycle wheels, jack-in-the boxes, model airplanes, and other childhood detritus. "I am going to burn in hell for this," Angel said. It wasn't her first abortion. More like her third. The first was at sixteen. She was twenty-two. She calculated that by the age of thirty, she would have killed seven babies.

"I'm a murderer," she said.

"Don't think like that," Dennis said. "Have another beer."

The clinic was full of couples. Framed posters hung on the walls—Georgia O'Keeffe flowers. Everyone stared at their shoes. One by one the girls and women were led away. Dennis expected to hear screams any minute, but there was only the sound of the fat girl behind the counter, sniffling and shuffling papers, and the radio playing softly—music from the seventies. It was the same station his boss listened to at work. When his boss took off, leaving Dennis to clean up and make cookies for the next day—that was all they sold, thirteen kinds of cookies— Dennis would roll down the corrugated metal door, change the station and crank up the music. He hadn't made it in much in the past couple of weeks, since meeting Angel. Maybe he would get fired. That was usually what happened.

A nurse came through a door that had a tacked-up chart about birth control on it. There were pictures of diaphragms, IUD's, condoms, a diagram of a penis showing what a vasectomy was, a thermometer for the rhythm method. The nurse called his name, and Dennis got up and followed her down a hall, to a room with a dozen or so beds in it. Angel was lying on one. Her eyes were closed.

"Hey," Dennis said.

She sat up, then got shakily to her feet, the nurse helping her.

"She'll be fine," the nurse said.

"They gave me Valium," Angel said. "They said, would you like something to relax? And they gave me Valium. I love Valium, " Angel said.

"Let's get out of here." Dennis took her arm and they walked slowly outside, where the sunlight hit them hard. They stood on the steps, blinking.

"Murderers," someone said. A tiny woman with a blotchy face emerged from the shadow of a tree and came hobbling towards them, leaning on a steel cane. "Murderers," she hissed.

"Fuck you," Angel said, and they headed for the car.


It was a while before they could fuck again, but they did everything else in the meantime. Angel insisted that Dennis go to work every day, so he wouldn't lose his job. She took a couple of days off from the bar and then went back. Things were settling down. The nights Angel worked, Dennis would come in and drink for free and play video poker and sometimes pool, though he wasn't any good at it. On her off nights she came to see him at the cookie stand after it closed, and would sit in the back room on a box of sugar while he baked. He told his roommates to find somebody else and moved his stuff into Angel's.

He didn't have much, just some clothes and a boom box and the war strategy games he liked to play. He had a map of Vietnam he spread out on Angel's threadbare living room rug, with NLF and ARVN and American troop movements represented by different-colored markers he moved around. His father had been in Nam and had talked about it sometimes, so a lot of the place names were familiar: Da Nang, Long Binh, Quang Tri. Dennis wished he had been there. Not with his father, but with other guys. Once he'd seen a group of Gulf War vets walking up and down Broadway, where the strip places were, and he tried to imagine himself walking with them, his hair cropped

14

short, looking as tough and world-weary as they did. His father had tripped a mine and gotten two toes of his left foot blown off, a deep divot gouged out of it. Dennis hadn't done shit. He'd moved von Blucher's soldiers toward Waterloo and MacArthur's forces across the 38th parallel, sitting stoned and crosslegged on his bedroom floor. He had a World War Two bomber jacket he'd bought in a thrift store. He had a nine-millimeter Smith & Wesson in a black case he hid on a high shelf in the closet, so Angel wouldn't know about it, and two envelopes of money he'd stolen from the cookie stand, a thousand dollars in each, that he put in Angel's underwear drawer.

"You shouldn't steal," Angel told him. "What if you get caught?"

"I won't get caught," Dennis said. "I'm smarter than he is."

They were watching TV—the siege of Stalingrad, in black and white. Tanks fired into a snowy haze. The German soldiers hardly moved, it was so cold. Angel didn't want to watch. She slid down under the covers and took Dennis into her mouth, trying to get him hard. Just when she was about to give up and scoot back out from under the blankets, he started responding.

"Keep sucking it," he said.

But Angel wanted to fuck. She pulled the blankets down. She got on top of him, moving against his hips, her hands on his chest to raise herself up.

They'd been using condoms since they had started up again. Dennis thought they should use one now, but the truth was he didn't like them, and Angel felt really good without that latex between them. He lay back and closed his eyes and let her do him, thinking of what it was like before he knew her—picking up stupid girls in clubs, girls he couldn't stand after he came in them, or jerking off by himself listening to tapes on the boom box, then feeling a big hole open up inside him like a bomb crater, feeling like a moony landscape where nothing could grow anymore because everything had been napalmed to shit.

He opened his eyes and there was Angel, her beautiful tits bouncing, her head thrown back. He reached for the thorns around her waist and pulled her harder into him, jamming her body against his. He was powerful as a king. He pulled her down to his chest and stroked her hair.

Where's that at? Angel thought, her ear against his pounding heart. I didn't even fucking come.


Milk chocolate chip, dark chocolate chip, either of those with macadamia nuts or just plain. Plain chocolate, oatmeal raisin, peanut butter. Peanut butter milk chocolate chip, peanut butter dark chocolate chip. Oatmeal milk chocolate chip, oatmeal dark chocolate chip. Chocolate milk chocolate chip, chocolate dark chocolate chip (Angel's favorite). Pepsi, Diet Pepsi, 7Up, Root Beer, Mr. Pibb. Dennis must have drunk gallons of Mr. Pibb. Lemonade or coffee. He drank a lot of coffee, too. He took a square of wax paper, reached for the cookies and put them in a paper bag with a picture of a happy-faced cookie on it. The Carpenters were on the radio, Karen Carpenter singing "We've Only Just Begun."

The stand was in the middle of the tourist district—a cheesy pier on the bay filled with ripoff restaurants and souvenir stores, a few mimes and clowns that worked the crowds. Dennis hated tourists. He hated how they spent their money on crap, like singing along with prerecorded pop songs with the vocals dropped out, and stupid hats and sweatshirts. He was saving his money. Before he met Angel, he didn't know what he was saving it for. Now he thought he'd like to take her someplace nice for a vacation. Club Med sounded cool. There were Club Meds all over the place. You could just lie around all day, eating and soaking up rays, and no one would hassle you.

He pocketed the next few sales; his boss was off hitting on the girls at the hot dog stand.

On his break he went out back of the buildings, where he could watch the seals. A bunch of them had settled in on an old, unused dock that was half-sunk into the bay; they lay there sunning themselves, glistening with salt water, massively at peace. Dennis lit a joint and took a deep drag. He thought about Angel, standing in front of the stove in a black undershirt, heating a can of Bean with Bacon soup. Angel at work, expertly freepouring shots, or raising the silver shaker high in the air when she made martinis. Angel in bed, her little mouth half-open, her eyes glittering up at him through the fringe of her black lashes, thick with mascara.

Back at work he decided to try stealing right under his boss's nose. It turned out to be easy; all he had to do was point out some girl walking by in shorts, and his boss would ogle her until she was out of sight, by which time Dennis had hit "No Sale" so the register would ring and taken the money. Dennis's boss was a fat pig. He reminded Dennis of his father—his boss was bald like his father, and had a nice-guy attitude Dennis knew was fake. His father had fucked anything that moved, including the babysitters. He'd stayed with Dennis's mother, pretending he loved her, patting her ass in the kitchen. Dennis used to follow him when he left the house. It gave him kind of a sick feeling, to see his dad kissing other women, going into their apartment buildings or houses or some motel, but he couldn't help it. He wondered what they thought when they saw his father naked, saw that mangled foot with its mess of scar tissue.

"Wouldn't you like to get into some of that?" his boss said.

Dennis looked. She must have been thirteen—tight jean shorts, a white halter you could see her baby tits through, white nylon knee socks. Scumbag.

"Nah," he said.


After work he drove downtown to Angel's bar.

"Oh, hi," she said, flipping her hair back. She looked tired. Dennis slid onto his usual stool.

"Why don't you pay for a drink, for once," Angel said.

"Okay, cool," Dennis said. He took out some of the money he'd stolen that day. It was mostly ones and fives. He usually waited until he got a big wad, then went to the bank and changed them into hundreds.

Angel was in a bad mood. She ignored Dennis, moving to the other end of the bar to talk to a couple of guys. They cheered her up, and pretty soon she was laughing with them. Dennis went over to the pool table, which was empty, and put a quarter in the slot. It took him quite a while to sink all the balls. The whole time, he heard Angel laughing.

When the guys left the bar, he followed them. They drove to a liquor store and came out with two big grocery bags. One of them put his bag on the hood of the car, lit a cigarette, and glanced across the street. Dennis slunk down below the steering wheel. Once his father had caught him spying—Dennis had tailed him from the bowling alley, where he'd picked up a girl, to a field behind the junior high. Dennis had been very careful after that. The two guys burned rubber leaving the liquor store and drove fast to another part of the city, where there were run-down houses set close together, with hardly any yards. They pulled up at one with a twisted mesh fence out front that looked like somebody had rammed into it.

Dennis parked farther down the street. He took the gun out of the glove compartment, where he'd kept it for the past couple of days. He walked back to the house and crept up to the window through a bunch of tall weeds. He looked in and saw a girl in a short shiny black skirt sitting on the couch, leaning forward to take a hit off a bong sitting on the coffee table. One of the guys went over and sat next to her and put his arm around her. They started making out.

Dennis pointed the gun.

"Bang," he whispered.

The couple on the couch writhed around. The girl's shirt was off now. Another girl came in and said something

Dennis couldn't hear. She started taking off her clothes, dancing around, and doing a theatrical strip-tease. She looked kind of drunk. It was like watching TV with the sound turned down—some late-night soft-core cable channel. Dennis felt queasy. He stumbled back to the car and drove aimlessly, the radio up as loud as he could stand it.

When he got home he hoped to find Angel in bed watching TV, but she wasn't there. He waited up, but she didn't come home until the next morning.

"So, like, what happened?" Dennis said.

"None of your business," Angel said. She was sick of Dennis coming in to the bar all the time, hanging around. Like she was supposed to entertain him or something. It was too much responsibility. I mean, she thought. Get a life.

"Where were you all night?" Dennis said. "I waited up. I was worried about you."

"What are you, my fucking parents?" Angel said.

Then she went to the bathroom and threw up.


A few nights later, Dennis dreamed about their baby. It was the size of a pint bottle, and it smiled at him. But then someone lit it on fire. He watched it burn, its little face crumpling like paper. He woke up sweating and turned to Angel, but she wasn't there.

At five a.m. Dennis was naked in the bathroom. He stood with his legs apart and his arms held straight out in front of him, pointing his gun at the mirror. He heard the key in the lock, heard Angel drop her big heavy purse to the floor. Then she was in the mirror, screaming at him.

"Where the fuck did you get that?" Angel said.

"I didn't want to freak you out," Dennis said. He put the gun down next to the sink.

"Is it loaded?"

"Fuck, no."

"Well, what are you doing with it?"

"Nothing." He gazed sullenly at a lipstick lying on the bathroom floor.

"You're crazy," Angel said.

He picked up the gun and tried to twirl it on his finger like they did in Westerns. Angel snorted and went into the bedroom. Dennis stood in the bathroom doorway and aimed the gun at her.

"Bang," he said. "You're dead."

"I don't think so," Angel said. "I just came back to get some clothes." She had to get ready for work. Dennis was in the way. He was always in the way lately; she'd turn from the refrigerator with a carton of Coffee-Mate, or be pulling a tray of Ore Ida Golden Crinkles from under the broiler, and he'd have snuck up behind her and be standing right there.

Angel went through her dresses, trying not to feel Dennis watching her. She had to be at work in half an hour. On Sundays she did the six a.m. club—the real goners, who had to have a couple of shots to steady their hands. Angel never drank until after five p.m. If she was working, she had whisky from a coffee cup. She was giving free drinks now to a guy named Mismo, who rode a Harley and wore black leather pants. They had screwed once right on the seat of the Harley.

Dennis had watched them from the bed of a pickup parked nearby. He had aimed the gun at Mismo's crotch, Angel's ass, the moon, a broken streetlight.

Dennis came into the bedroom.

"I love you, Angel," he said.

"Oh, please," Angel said. "I have to go to work."

"Just let me put it in," Dennis said. "Just for a second."

"No."

"Please."

"NO." Angel had her dress on already.

Dennis went into Angel's closet and rummaged on the shelf until he found one of the round happy-faced cookie tins he'd taken from work, where the clip of bullets was hidden, wrapped in a piece of blue felt. He took out the clip and shoved it into the gun. He was standing among

Angel's dresses and blouses, inhaling the sweet flowery scent of her perfume.

He came out of the closet. Angel was sitting on the bed, pulling on her pantyhose.

"It's loaded now," he said.

"Go away, Dennis." She drew the nylons up her legs, stood and lifted her dress to adjust them.

"Lie down," Dennis said.

Angel put her shoes on. "Grow up, asshole," she said. "It's over." She picked up her purse and slung it over her shoulder.

After she was gone he lay down on the bed and watched TV. He put the gun beside him on a pillow. He watched the Today show, and then the Jetsons and the Flintstones. He turned off the TV and went into the living room to his map of Vietnam and sat down, studying it. Hue was in ruins, the buildings destroyed, the big park a smoldering mess. Hue was going to fall. Eventually, Saigon was, too. It was all pointless. People had died for nothing. Innocent people. Stupid soldiers. Women in rice paddies. Before that, people in concentration camps. Babies.

I have killed babies, Dennis thought.

He felt better and worse. He went and got the gun and put it to his head.

"Bang," he said. He took the clip out and set it next to the gun, on Angel's dresser. He put on his black fatigues, his T-shirt with the picture of William Burroughs on it, and his combat boots. He opened Angel's underwear drawer to get his money; the envelopes smelled of rose sachet. He stuffed them in his green canvas duffel along with a few clothes. There wasn't anything else he needed. In the living room he kicked at the game on the floor, scattering the armies to the corners of the room. He picked up his boom box, then set it back down. He decided he had enough to carry, wherever the fuck he was going.

# *inside out*

Today I can't move. Loren was coming over with his truck, but it broke down, it will be tomorrow, tomorrow he will come with a truck and move me. I have been living among boxes, boxes in the kitchen which are full of things to put food on, drinks in, there is a box of cookbooks explaining what I am to do. In the bedroom are more boxes, a trunk containing very white sheets with a flower pattern, a small accordion file of letters. There is a bag of things. I don't know where I will put it, maybe in a suitcase. In the bag are private things—a vibrator, lotion, handcuffs, ads for magazines and videotapes showing sexual acts. I masturbate looking at these, though I do not order the magazines or tapes, I look at the very small cunts and cocks and assholes and excite myself.

I have several things to do today, several errands which will take up the time. Time is a problem because there are not always errands to fill it, or there are errands but I can't do them. The biggest problem is leaving the apartment, deciding what clothes are appropriate and actually putting them on and walking down the stairs and into the street. In the street, something could happen. A man might follow me, even in broad daylight, and when I walked faster he would too, and I would turn the wrong way, into a street where there were no more houses, only a big blank warehouse and a store that used to be an upholstery shop. He would pull me into an alley, behind a dumpster, and tell me he was going to kill me. I would have to lie down on some smashed cardboard boxes, my head on the ground, gravel digging into my cheek. I would stare at a paper cup, a medium-sized cup from McDonald's with a plastic lid on top and a clear straw sticking out of it, and listen to the things he said, things I had heard before. Little whore, he said. I can tell you want it. Dirty little girl. I would lie there and not move or speak, even after he got up off of me, even when he was gone.

I have a list of things to do. Today, for example, I have to go to Walgreen's and fill two prescriptions. Walgreen's is one block away, so maybe I will be able to do this. Of course there are people I must pass to get there. I tell myself that they will be nice people, but I don't know. Sometimes it is hard to tell just by looking, sometimes you can be fooled. I will have to find just the right outfit; if it is cold or foggy I can wear the long dark-purple coat from Salvation Army. Also today I have to buy coffee, that is second on my list. The coffee store is around the corner, and the woman who works there is very friendly towards me. I do not have to be nervous about walking in, choosing the right beans, taking out the money and waiting while she grinds them and then giving her the money and taking the change from her hand. In some stores this process of exchanging money is excruciating. If there is a male clerk, even a teenaged boy just a few

24

years younger than me, I am afraid he will slowly and deliberately brush my palm with the tips of his fingers, and I will not be able to take my hand away. I always try to have pennies and nickels so I can give the correct amount. Walgreen's, the coffee store. This is not too much to ask of myself. Everything is packed and ready to go; there is no reason to stay in today.

I look at myself in the mirror, which has been taken off the wall and leans against an emptied bureau. My thighs are slightly open, dark hairs curl around my cunt. In the mirror I am flat, like a magazine picture. I slip my finger inside where it is wet and warm and contained, and contract the muscles so my finger is held tightly. Tomorrow Loren will come with his truck, tomorrow he will put his cock where my finger is. Loren says that when we live together, I won't be so afraid. Loren is older, he says he will take care of me. When I curl up in bed he will be there, breathing softly. He will move inside me like this, back and forth. Loren is always careful and patient. Sometimes he will put his mouth between my legs and stay there for what seems like hours; he goes on trying to make me come past the point when he should give up. Finally I push him away, when there is a large wet ring on the sheet from my juices and his saliva. I have explained to Loren that since the rape, I can't come except when I am alone. Masturbating, I rub myself and imagine being with him in his loft bed, so close to the ceiling. I see the small cement grains of the ceiling as pores in someone's skin. My orgasm builds and builds, then is over in a second. I have to go to the bathroom. I have to fill two prescriptions at Walgreen's and go to the coffee store. I have to go down the stairs.


Sasha calls. Are you okay, Fran? he says.

Yes, Sasha. But I am going out soon, I have things to take care of. I'm moving in with Loren tomorrow.

Let me come over, Sasha says. I can't work, the piece is going nowhere. I want to see you.

I don't know. I'm on my way out the door.

I have on a sleeveless white jockey undershirt, striped underwear. I have put on purple eye shadow, mascara, black lipstick. The turquoise stud and the gold monkey in my left ear, a lacquered circle in my right. This is as far as I got, before sitting down and lighting a cigarette. I smoked and looked at myself, looked at the whore in the mirror. I put on a tape Sasha gave me, a performance of some music he wrote, and watched the whore dance the way they do at the Lusty Lady, where Sasha took me once. We stood close together in the small booth while the women moved their hips on the other side of the glass, smiling down at us, dancing to loud music under bright stage lights. After smoking the cigarette I felt dizzy and hungry, but there was nothing to eat because I had not been to the grocery store; the grocery store is over three blocks away, so I do not go there often. Also I only get a few items each time—cups of yogurt, pints of one-percent milk, boxes of animal crackers. Small things that will not weigh me down. I got into bed and lay on top of the quilt, listening to the music.

Is that my piece playing in the background? Sasha says.

Yes. I'm just listening to it for the first time. I'm going to lie here and enjoy it for a while.

I thought you were going out.

I am. As soon as your piece is finished.

Please, Fran. Let me come over.

Bring something to eat, then. I haven't been to the store and I'm starving.


Sasha tells me to get on my knees on the kitchen floor and handcuffs me to a leg of the table. He sits cross-legged beside me and feeds me crackers with paté and Camembert, slices of peach, a white chocolate truffle. He feeds me with one hand, and with the other he finger-fucks me. The tape player is on the kitchen table. A string quartet is playing a suite of Thelonius Monk's music, pieces I have heard Sasha play on the piano. When the first side ends Sasha stands up and flips the tape over.

Do you have any K-Y?

In a box in the bathroom.

My ass is very tight and tensed. I take deep breaths, and he gives me his hand to bite. I bite deeper and deeper, wanting to draw blood. He takes his hand away and slaps me hard on the ass.

Ouch. You're hurting me.

Isn't that what you want?

Yes.

I get excited when Sasha hurts me. I don't come, but sometimes I feel as though I might. While we are fucking I feel ashamed of myself; I am betraying Loren with one of his friends. Loren is the one who introduced us, and who suggested that Sasha might want to rent my place so Loren and I could move in together. I do things with Sasha that Loren would probably never think of doing.

Loren is so kind, so patient with me. He wants to protect me, but he can't. He can't be with me every minute. There are always opportunities; this is what I learned as a child. Your mother may have to go work the night shift at the hospital, even if you cry hysterically, even if you wrap your arms around her knees, and your stepfather will pry you off and carry you into your room. I'll give you something to cry about, he'll say. You may have to go to the doctor, and he will take off lunch and pick you up at school and drive you to a parking space in a dark corner of the mall garage, far from the other cars and the people going in and out of the big glass doors. A man may follow you for blocks, blocks of ordinary storefronts, flowers on the sidewalk, women pushing strollers, a little boy with a silver balloon. There are places you can't see, holes you might fall into.

Sasha grabs my hair and jerks my head back. God, I love you, he says, and comes.

The men on the first floor are making love, groaning loudly. I wonder which one of them is taking it up his ass—the one who keeps the parakeet, or the one with the thin black mustache. I often eavesdrop on my neighbors. I want to know what goes on, what is behind the faces I see in front of the building, faces that smile at me and seem to wish me well. There are airwells, little closed-in alleys, between my building and the ones on each side. The smallest sounds carry. There are also a couple of windows I can see into. In one of them, on the first floor next door, I can see a kitchen sink. Usually I see a woman's hands over the sink, making orange juice in a large pitcher, or scrubbing pans. She and her husband have two little girls, who make a lot of noise playing and then get yelled at by their parents. Late at night I often lie awake and listen, to hear if there might be a small sound from one of the girls, the sound she would make waking up from some dream to feel a hand between her legs, her nightgown being pulled up to cover her face. Sometimes I don't sleep all night.

Through another window, level with my bathroom, I can see a bedroom. I can't see the bed, though I can hear the man and woman making love. Sometimes I catch sight of one of them naked, which excites me, especially if it is the woman. I stare at her breasts, so different from mine—smaller, the nipples pinker, more pointed, like little arrow tips. Her whole body is like cream, her cunt hair very blonde and sparse, her ass too large and veined with stretch marks. I have a pair of binoculars to watch her. Sometimes she stands there for several minutes, apparently looking into a mirror; I see her in profile, leaning forward to peer at her face, then turning sideways so her back is to me and looking over her shoulder. Once the man came up beside her as she was studying herself and rubbed himself against her, and then pushed inside. I watched them, the man grunting, the woman's head thrown back. I watched her come.

When I see myself fully dressed in the mirror I am reassured that nothing is wrong with me. But really, I am afraid that the person in the mirror is not me, that she is only a picture that moves when I move, and disappears when I turn my back. She goes away, where I can't find her, and leaves me here.

Loren always turns out the lights when we make love, but Sasha deliberately exposes me and places me in humiliating positions. When we are out together he will sometimes push me against a wall and kiss me and put his hand inside my coat or down my pants. One night, outside a bar, he pushed me against the post of a street lamp and lifted my dress. Even though he opened his coat to hide us, it must have been obvious to anyone who passed what we were doing. I closed my eyes and put my face in his shoulder, feeling miserable and ashamed and crying softly, but he would not stop. Sasha tells me he is going to turn me inside-out, as if that will help. He doesn't understand that I already feel that way.

One of the men on the first floor has just shouted, *Oh shit, oh shit, oh Jesus.* Sasha left an hour ago, to go back to his piano and work on a score for a ballet. I called Loren, to find out what time he would be coming tomorrow. He wasn't there so I left the question on his machine. I told him I might not be in when he called back, that I had some errands to take care of. I walked around the apartment a couple of times, lay back down on the kitchen floor and masturbated, and then I took a long shower. I imagined the street, the dark places where something could happen, even with people around, even if you covered yourself up. I got dressed, put makeup on.

I just can't do it.


I stand at the window and watch people go by below me. Two women stroll hand in hand, a boy walks a bicycle too big for him. I open the window and sit on the sill, my legs dangling. The day is sunny, starting to cool off a little with a damp breeze. I am on the third floor, it is unlikely that anyone would look up at me. So I am surprised when a man with an unruly golden retriever pulls the dog's leash hard at the corner, stops to wait for the light and glances up. He shades his eyes, looking, and then he waves. I wave back, too startled to withdraw into the safety of the room. I think he must know me. But he isn't one of my neighbors, or anyone I recognize. He's just a stranger. He looks right at me, and smiles, and I realize that he can't really see me, he has no idea who I am.

# *surgeries*

In the middle of boiling water for tea, drunk on whisky, she decided to call her ex-husband, whom she hadn't called for a year and two months and three days, not counting all the calls to hear his voice on the machine or to hang up if he answered. She had heard that he'd moved, and she thought she would ask him for his new address just in case she needed to drive by in the middle of the night sometime to stare at the dark windows and wonder if he was with some other woman and what he said to her when they made love, and to remember all the things he used to say during sex that she still could not believe he was no longer saying. Now he was saying that he was still her husband, legally at least, because he couldn't bring himself to file the final papers. I didn't want you to get them around your birthday, he said.

And then there were the holidays, and then Valentine's Day. I never filed them, he said. I still love you, why did you leave me? she said. It's been a hard time, he said, two more surgeries on my wrist and I'm still in pain, they're going to have to fuse it and meanwhile I need to get a job; I'm broke, he said, and she was crying and he was saying I think about you all the time, I want to see you and she said, You know what will happen, we'll just destroy each other again and in the kitchen the forgotten kettle was shooting steam into the air with a piercing shriek she finally heard, Oh God I've got to go, she said, I guess you didn't change your number, but can I have your new address? I haven't moved, he said.

# the gift

I find a dildo on the street: thick and slightly curved, flesh-colored. It looks so convincing that for a second I think it is a real penis, and I feel a sense of vertigo. It's brand-new, wrapped in white tissue which has ripped open. There's a thin blue-and-white-striped ribbon tied around it, and red scotch tape with little Christmas tree designs holding the corners.

I look around to see if there is someone nearby who might have dropped it. The street is full of people entering and leaving stores, carrying oddly-shaped packages, or dragging enormous bags full of gifts, no doubt intended for loved ones, yes, it is clear that everyone but me has loved ones to buy for. The dildo could belong to anyone. It looks elegant and expensive and forlorn, lying there so vulnerably, perhaps about to be stepped on, trampled underfoot, a smudged heel mark left on the still-pristine tissue; perhaps it will be kicked aside, to lie all night beside a garbage can, or even placed inside it with the reek of old hamburger wrappers to which well-chewed gray gum clings. I can't bear these thoughts; I bend down to cradle the object in my hand. I think for a minute of its rightful owner—perhaps some woman like me, a woman who is lonely, isolated in fact, a woman who has no one to be with at Christmas. Maybe she bought herself a present, a present she would wait until Christmas morning to open; maybe she would take it to bed and close her eyes and moan and rock back and forth on it saying "John, John" (for that is his name, the man who walked out on me at the start of the holiday shopping season, leaving me devastated, perhaps even suicidal, who knows what I may do next), and then she would come, her legs stiffening, her juices flowing, and she would begin to cry afterwards and perhaps fling it across the room with a curse; but now I have deprived her of all that, I have picked it up and put it into the pocket of my long black coat and hurried home with it.

Now it sits—or stands, rather—on the dresser, freed of its wrappings. It glows in the light of the lamp, its veins seem to pulse, a rosy aura suffuses it. I take off my clothes and approach it, something seems to radiate from it—a sense of ease and power, a kind of self-satisfaction, a kind of . . . lust—yes, it is clearly lust I feel. I seize it in my hand, I fall to the floor with it and writhe around, it throbs under my palm, swells and hardens as I pump it faster and faster. My orgasm builds until I explode all over the rug; come spurts from me, one spurt, another; I lie exhausted holding it in my hand, I pass out from the sheer pleasure of it.

I wake up, not knowing how long I have been unconscious. Maybe minutes, but maybe years; I could be an old woman, finished with sex forever, content to sit on a sagging plaid couch and stare at the television in an ugly room with no visitors day after day; I eat candy bars from the vending machine, at night I take pills and lie awake listening to the radiator and the nurses' shoes going by my door and the person in the next room trying to breathe with his weak collapsed lungs. I stagger to my feet, feeling strange and dizzy; I look in the full-length mirror and see that I am not an old woman at all; I am a young man.

I have a large penis, thick and slightly curved, dark hair around my balls. I yank at it and feel it at the base of my belly; I look at myself in horror. I would gladly turn into something else—a werewolf, a vampire; I would happily be like Gregor Samsa and live out the rest of my life as a dung beetle. But I am a man. And already, as I look at myself, the horror begins to fade; I can no longer think or feel anything but—yes, again it is lust I feel; I touch the head of my penis and it quivers, it longs to dive into the bedsheets and thrust, over and over, it takes me with it, I come all over the sheets yelling and thrashing about.

Afterwards I sleep deeply. I wake the next morning and think it has been a dream, perhaps I am delusional, perhaps the doctor was right after all and I should begin taking Prozac, but truthfully I feel better than I have in weeks, and besides I have a hard-on; I lie there dreamily pulling on my penis, and come again in the sheets which are already a little stiff and sticky. I think of doing the laundry, it has been so long since I have washed the sheets, or my clothes, or cleaned the apartment; I have been so depressed over John's leaving. But I do not want to clean today. No, I want to take a shower and eat a large breakfast and take my penis out into the world.

Now the streets look different, the shoppers so hurried, so pathetic in their desperate efforts to find just the right gift. I walk confidently, feeling my penis bulge against the zipper of my jeans; it is my companion, I will never feel lonely again, it will accompany me everywhere. I thank God for this gift of a penis, my beautiful wonderful penis, tucked so cozily inside my silk underwear, nestled like a little wren; I see an attractive man and the wren begins to grow talons, it lifts its great wings and follows the man with its fierce eagle eyes; it wants to swoop down and carry him off to my apartment and feast on him for hours.

I follow the man down the street, into a store where he fingers scarves, looks at expensive earrings, takes down pretty kimonos from a rack. I remember that I am a man, too, and suddenly a wave of revulsion rises in me; the thought of dragging him home with me is crushed and drowned by the wave crashing over it. I am normal, I say to myself, normal; there is nothing wrong with me, I have never been a woman or wanted to make love to a man, I must wipe all that from my mind—especially the image of sucking on a penis, the joy of taking it into my mouth, licking the clear liquid that forms a bright drop at the tip, swallowing the slightly bitter fluid as I kneel before John, as he strokes my hair and says Baby, oh baby—I must erase all that.

I hurry from the store, and now I see the women, their breasts bulging inside sweaters, or hidden under coats, their asses moving just ahead of me like beacons to guide me; I think of their cunts and their smells, their soft inviting mouths. The eagle circles and circles, hunger gnaws at its belly, and now a kind of terror: I must find a woman, a woman who will have me, suddenly my penis is profoundly lonely and cold and sad.

I go into a bar, and the terror is greater; there are women here, all around me in twos and threes; my penis is about to leap from my pants. I want to go up to one of them, to lean her back over a table and plunge into her, but I must stop myself; I drink beer after beer to quell my anxiety, to try and think of a way to do this politely. I stumble to the back of the bar, into the men's room, stand at the urinal and watch the arc of piss, golden and fragrant, and I am so fascinated by it I forget about the women. I go into a stall and jerk off, sitting on the toilet, and then emerge calm and in control once more. I return to the bar and continue to drink. I talk to no one, I think bitterly about my life, my past lovers, I resolve not to ever love anyone again; somewhere in the deepest recesses of my brain I remember who I am, I know that something is wrong, but it no longer matters. I get gloriously drunk, so drunk that everything goes black and disappears...

I wake up in a strange, but prettily decorated, room. I am lying in a canopy bed, tiny lights are strung around it, blinking on and off; Bing Crosby is singing "White Christmas," and I can smell sugar cookies baking somewhere. I want to reach between my legs to see if I still have my penis, but I can't move my arm very far. Perhaps I have had a stroke, and there is no hope I will regain my bodily functions; I am in a hospice, no one will visit me but volunteers doing their Zen practice, who will sit beside me to experience dying close up and tell me I must learn to let go. Forget John, they will say; life is but a dream, they are saying, or someone is singing; yes, a little girl is singing "Row, Row, Row Your Boat," in a high, pleasant voice. Now she is standing over my bed, but her face is huge, impossibly huge; surely I am dying, and this is the angel of death, wearing enormous wings and a white gown and holding a plain wooden wand in one hand, a glittery silver star stuck to one end of it. She reaches down for me, and lifts me, naked, into the air. She sets me on the dresser, and I see in the mirror that I am supposed to be female, I have long slim legs, a tiny waist, but I have no nipples on my otherwise perfect breasts and nothing between my legs but a sort of hinge, no sex at all anymore. I try to open my rosebud mouth to scream, but it is painted shut; it smiles happily back at me. "Merrily, merrily, merrily," the little girl sings, and begins to brush my hair.

# a brief history of condoms

1. *Origins of the American Condom*

The so-called American Condom (*Prophylacticus Americanus*) began behind the counters of druggists, springing to life in the dust and dark among prescription bottles.[1] In the diaspora which followed, some migrated into the air-conditioned light of Walgreens and Thriftys, others to the flickering fluorescent haze of convenience stores. Still others settled behind glass cabinets in large grocery chains. The most colorful varieties live crowded in baskets on the

---

[1] The largely discredited "Big O Theory," first developed by Holstein, posits a divine origin, to wit: that the universe was originally the size and shape of a gigantic, cosmically conscious condom, which masturbated itself and exploded into particles which ripped it apart and sent particles streaming outward into space. There are still some elements of the scientific community who claim that there is an inner condom in each of us,

counters of medical clinics. Condoms thrive in great numbers throughout the continent of North America, and tend to be concentrated in large cities. Fundamentalist Christians and the occasional zealous Catholic have decreased their numbers slightly, but the overall impact of such predation has been insignificant on the population as a whole.

2. *Life Cycle of the Condom*
A condom is a simple one-celled organism which appears, at first look, to be round and flat. When released from its foil "nest" and massaged, it changes its shape into a sock-like, membraneous creature which clings to human flesh—specifically, the male sexual organ. Condoms have a symbiotic relationship with humans; sperm released during human sexual activity is caught and eaten by the condom, allowing the condom to reproduce itself. Having fulfilled its evolutionary purpose, the condom then shrivels and dies. The fetus, or "conda," microscopic in size at this point, becomes airborne until it finds a suitable "nest," slips inside it and gestates in the warmth and protection the foil offers. A condom may lie dormant in its nest for years, but life outside the nest last from only a few minutes to half an hour or so. [2] It is fair to say that these brief moments, however, are by far the most gratifying; condoms have been observed to burst from sheer pleasure, and occasionally to squirm off of the male penis and travel excitedly upwards into the interior regions of the partner's body. [3]

remnant of the Great Rubber, and that we are reabsorbed into it at the end of earthly life. It's interesting to note that numerous mythologies of so-called primitive peoples offer variants of this proposition.

[2] The briefest known lifespan is .078 seconds; the longest, evidenced by a videotape of pornographic artist Jackoff Holmes, was well over an hour. Research has indicated that short-lived condoms tend to exhibit a high level of anxiety, whereas the longest-living emit alpha waves—an indication that, in human terms, these latter condoms tend to "stop and smell the roses," i.e. the odors of anal or vaginal secretions.

[3] Emergency Room records indicate that a small percentage of patients seek treatment, but the incidence is undoubtedly more frequent, according to anecdotal sources.

3. *Common Uses of the Condom*
There are many valuable uses of the condom beyond
the aforementioned use in sexual activity. Condoms may
be filled with water and dropped from high windows to
terrify old people, or loaded with jello and thrown at parties. They may be blown up like balloons. The flavored
variety, once the lubricant is wiped away, is favored for
eating by adolescent girls. Condoms may be used in de-
laying sexual activity, as in, " I won't fuck you if I have to
wear that thing on my dick."⁴ Such a statement may have
unfortunate results if the condom is then discarded, as it
will simply dry up and die without reproducing itself.
Condoms are dependent on human males, some of whom
have an ambivalent relationship with them, and see them
at best as a necessary evil.

4. *Inner Life of the Condom*
It is hard to ascertain whether a condom is capable of
the emotions you and I regard as a part of sentient life.
Does a condom experience depression, or fear death?
Does it have a soul? If so, then we must examine carefully our treatment of this useful creature. Should it, for
example, be so quickly relegated to the floor beside the
bed, or the trash in the bathroom, or the weeds of the
vacant lot? Perhaps our responsibility should extend to
a decent burial, a few words said to mark the passing of
our pleasure-seeking, short-lived friend. Perhaps it loves
the woman whose vaginal walls drench it for a few minutes, or the man whose anus contracts around it. Perhaps it realizes that such bliss must soon, too soon, turn
into pain and diminishment, into the awful isolation of
the separate self. If the condom could speak, what truths
might it tell us, privy as it is to some of our most intimate
moments?

---

⁴ In the late twentieth century, this statement is an indication of gross
stupidity on the part of the speaker. The best response to such an attitude
is probably, "Go fuck yourself."

### 5. *One Condom's Story*

She carries me in her purse. She intends to be faithful, but just in case, she wants to be prepared. She is on a long trip, away from her lover. She meets a man who delights her, who is clever and interesting. He puts his hand on her hip as they are walking. They find a bar and drink until they can hardly stand up, then stagger to a hotel room. I hear them laughing and giggling, hear the rustle of clothes and good intentions being rapidly discarded. There is a blinding light as I am freed, feeling the cool air wash deliciously over me, and then I am lost in sensation, nothing matters but this, it is glorious, I am stretched taut, headed for that beautiful deadly opening; I go in and in. My head floods with sperm and I gorge myself, losing consciousness, and when I wake I find myself flushed down the pipes, along the sewers and out into the great river of the unborn, riding the currents down to the mothering sea. [5]

### 6. *Social Organization of Condom Communities*

There are many classes—one might even say castes—in the condom community. Brightly colored and flavored condoms are usually ostracized by those with a more uniform look and packaging. These second-class citizens are more likely to attempt to form what we can only call personal attachments with other condoms. Through a process known as "nest-ripping," two separate condoms may leak their lubricants and form a sort of gluey mass which causes the nests to bind to each other. They then become unfit for human use and hence unable to reproduce, so why this occurs remains an evolutionary mystery. [6]

---

[5] The account is fictional; see Christopher Peckerwood's *I Am A Condom.* There are no authenticated stories of condoms speaking or writing their views, though apocryphal ones abound. Various people have claimed to be kidnapped by condoms from outer space, or to hear the voices of dead condoms speaking to them.

[6] For further readings see "Nest-ripping: Nature or Nurture?" in *Scientific American;* "Nest-Rippers, Menace to Society," ibid.; and the San Francisco journal *Honey, Let It Rip.*

7. *In Conclusion: A Personal Note*

There is much still to learn about this deceptively simple creature. I have here attempted the briefest outline of serious study and research. My own fascination began, perhaps, when as I boy I unrolled my first condom and jerked off into it, finding it a much neater method than rutting into the sheets my mother would have to wash. I have, frankly, never encountered a human body which gave me as much pleasure as the simple, unassuming condom, always eager to please, ready to take my jism and lap it up deliriously, then lie peacefully hanging from my penis while I relaxed with a cigarette. Several times during these jottings I have stopped to "denest" and massage one of the little creatures, to slip it over me and caress it, to squeeze and pull until we were both deliciously sated. [7] I confess to you now that I love them, that I think of nothing but their moist dripping bodies, that at night they come to me in my dreams, they hover over me and smile, and at last begin to speak.

[7] I can't get enough. Desire is endless. Sometimes I want to fuck everything in sight. I want to fuck the sheets, the trees outside my window, the men and women passing on the streets below; I want that ecstasy that only sex provides, the loss of self and finding of it, the *petit-morte* that tells me there is no true death, there is only connection and ceaseless change, there is only love against the darkness surrounding us, we are all ripped from the nest, helpless and exposed together; oh friends and colleagues, it all comes down to this: So many condoms. So little time.

# survivors

He and his lover were down to their last few T-cells and arguing over who was going to die first. He wanted to be first because he did not want to have to take care of his lover's parrot or deal with his lover's family, which would descend on their flat after the funeral, especially the father who had been an Army major and had tried to beat his son's sexual orientation out of him with a belt on several occasions during adolescence; the mother, at least, would be kind but sorrowful, and secretly blame him, the survivor—he knew this from her letters, which his lover had read to him each week for the past seven years. He knew, too, that they all—father, mother, two older brothers—would disapprove of their flat, of the portrait of the two of them holding hands that a friend had painted and which hung over the bed, the Gay Freedom Day poster in the bathroom, all the absurd little knickknacks like the small plastic wind-up penis that hopped around on two feet; maybe, after his lover died, he would put some things away, maybe he would even take the parrot out of its cage and open the window so it could join the wild ones he'd heard of, that nested in the palm trees on Dolores Street, a whole flock of bright tropical birds apparently thriving in spite of the chilly Bay Area weather—he would let it go, fly off, and he would be completely alone then; dear God, he thought, let me die first, don't let me survive him.

# *gas*

Deena sits on the hood of a truck sunk to its fenders in weeds and dying sunflowers in the field next to the gas station. The sun has made the metal burning hot; the heat pulses through her pajama bottoms, and she tries to see how long she can stand it before having to jump down. Bees hum by her ears and swarms of gnats hang in the air between her and where her mother stands leaning against a squat red Coke machine, holding a can to her forehead the way she has often held a washcloth wrung in cold water that Deena has brought her. Deena's mother looks like a model, with her long blonde hair and tight jeans and halter top. She is only twenty-three. The small silver hoop in her pierced navel glints in the sun. She is still as a statue, staring across the two-lane road at nothing Deena can see. There is only a broken wood fence

47

someone has strung wire across to repair, and a couple of dusty-looking brown horses grazing beside it, twitching their black tails once every few minutes at the flies.

Her mother had wakened her in the dark that morning, whispering that they had to go and telling Deena to be quiet. Deena had time to grab several Barbies and her stuffed pink pig, a present for her birthday last month. Instead of a cake, her mother had made seven chocolate cupcakes with a red spiraled candle in each one. She had set the kitchen table with a lace tablecloth, and put out paper plates with pictures of balloons on them. There were balloons all over the kitchen, too, shiny silver ones that hovered along the ceiling, their thin colorful ribbons hanging down so you had to push them aside, walking through them. Deena's mother had let her blow out the candles and eat two cupcakes before dinner. But then her mother spilled some gravy on her dress, and the baked potatoes got overdone and hard—she dragged Deena to the stove and made her feel one, a hot stone wrapped in a dishcloth—and then her mother took the rest of the cupcakes and threw them one by one against the wall or through the door that led to the living room.

The pig had a zipper in its belly where three piglets usually were, but that morning they were scattered over her bedroom, and Deena couldn't find them. She took her favorite blue button-down sweater that had her name stitched in white on the right breast, and a Pez dispenser, and she wasn't sure what else; her mother was by now yanking her out by one arm, and she just scooped up whatever was on the floor into the K-Mart bag she was using as a suitcase. She dragged it behind her down the hallway and out the apartment door, and then into the old elevator that had a noisy metal gate you had to pull open before stepping inside.

The rasping of the gate sounded to Deena like fireworks going off, but their apartment door remained closed. Jackson must still be sleeping. Jackson was her mother's boyfriend. He had tufts of black hair sprouting on his back, and he had tattoos: a giant phoenix spreading its wings across his chest, a tiger snarling on his right shoulder , and a dagger on his arm that he could make move by clenching and unclenching his fist. Deena liked Jackson because he didn't argue with her mother when she got drunk and yelled and threw things, the way the boyfriends before Jackson had done. He just got drunk himself, growing quieter and slower and more clumsy, until he lay down on the couch or the floor and passed out. In the morning, Deena would get up to watch cartoons on the TV in the living room and Jackson would be lying there, his right arm flung over his forehead, a dead cigarette and a burnhole somewhere near his left hand. She would turn the TV on low and scoot right up in front of it. When she got hungry she'd go in the kitchen and fix herself some Frosted Flakes or Sugar Smacks, and bring the bowl of cereal back to the TV.

She has probably missed all the morning cartoons by now; the sun is dead center in the sky. Deena squints up at it, then squeezes her eyes shut to see the black and violet sunspots. She feels like an egg frying in an iron skillet. Finally she jumps down and stands a minute, staring at a sunflower face drooping over right in front of her. Tiny black bugs crawl along the shriveling petals. From here she can't see her mother anymore, just part of the gray cement of the gas station's side wall. Everything else is hidden by the truck. The fender is rusted, and she scrapes off a few flakes with a fingernail.

"Deena," her mother calls, not very loudly.

Deena thinks about walking away into the field and lying down in the warm dirt, hidden from everything but the sunflowers. She thinks of her mother, frantically searching for her the way she searches for her keys, tearing up the place until she finds them. Her mother would trample the flowers, grinding them under her heels. She would smack Deena in the face, or pinch her on the arm, a long, hard pinch that left a bruise. Or she would just kick her, to punish her. Often, at home, after her mother

49

had gotten after her, Deena would go into her closet and curl up in the back, next to a broken humidifier and a pile of clothes she'd outgrown. Eventually her mother would come in, get down beside her, hold her too tightly and cry. Deena's mother is too young to have a child. She is doing the best she can, and Deena is not helping. Deena knows her mother's troubles by heart. She is her mother's precious baby, her darling girl, and she is also a weight around her neck, a stone dragging her down, the reason she will never again have any fun in life.

Reluctantly Deena comes around the side of the truck. Her mother is pacing back and forth in front of the Coke machine, still holding the can to her forehead.

"You want a soda?" her mother says.

"Okay," Deena says.

Their car is on the lift in the garage, and a man is fooling around underneath it, occasionally banging on something with a hammer. A radio plays loud rock music, the same kind her mother listens to at night, when Deena is trying to sleep. She sometimes puts toilet paper in her ears, but during the school year she can't do that, since she might not hear her alarm clock in the morning. Her mother is not a morning person, so she can't help Deena get up or get ready for school. After the music an announcer comes on and gives the weather for Minneapolis and Saint Paul. He says it is supposed to rain, which Deena finds hard to believe. All around them the sky is a flat, boring blue. She wonders how close they are to those cities.

"Mommy," she says. "Are we still in Wisconsin?"

"No, baby," her mother says.

"Are we going home when the car gets fixed?"

Her mother doesn't answer. She puts some change into the Coke machine, and a can thunks down. "There's your soda," she says. "Drink it and be quiet now." She fishes out a pack of Marlboro Lights from her big black purse, then scrounges for a lighter. She flicks it several times, but it only gives a series of quick sparks. "Shit," she says,

50

and throws it toward a trash can set between the two gas pumps. It hits the paper towel dispenser and falls. "Goddamn shit," she says.

Deena sits on the curb in front of the gas station's plate glass window. Yellow plastic quarts of oil are lined up in a neat row in the window, making her think of targets at the carnival you have to shoot for a prize—a pinwheel or long purple stuffed snake or big panda bear, depending on how many you shoot. She went once to the carnival with her mother and another boyfriend, Don, who won her the panda bear. That had gotten left behind on the previous move. Deena tries to remember Don's face, but all she remembers is that one of his hands was littler than the other and curled in, like a claw—that was the hand that held the rifle at the carnival. Before, when they were living with him, her mother had warned her never to talk about Don's hand. But after they left her mother would make fun of it, curling her own in imitation. When Deena went to the carnival they had been living in Tiffin, Ohio, which they left for Dayton, and after Dayton there was Cleveland. The boyfriend in Cleveland was named Tommy. Tommy had woken up when they were about to leave and come out onto the front stoop in his boxers, and her mother had driven the car up over the yellow grass of the front yard and straight toward him. At the last minute she stepped on the brakes, throwing Deena forward against her shoulder harness and back hard against the seat. Tommy had just stood there, his hands at his sides, looking at them. Then he started to cry, and her mother backed the car down to the driveway and they left. Deena was glad they left, because Tommy had called her into the bathroom one morning when her mother was gone, and shown her his penis and tried to get her to touch it. After that they lived in Menomonie, Wisconsin, with Jackson, and now they are who knows where.

"Menomonie," Deena says softly. She had said it over and over when they first arrived there, liking the sound of the word. "Menomonie Menomonie Menomonie," she says now. Soon it starts sounding like "Menamenamen"; she keeps it up until her mother slaps her hard on the side of her head.

"Quit that yammering," her mother says.

Deena's ear burns. She put her hand up to it, then quickly puts it down. "That didn't hurt," she says.

"Oh, honey," her mother says. She puts her can of Coke to Deena's ear; the cold is soothing. "I just react sometimes," she says. "I don't know what the hell is wrong with me."

"There's nothing to do around here," Deena says.

"I have an idea," her mother says. "Here, give me that." She takes Deena's soda and sets it on the curb, along with her own. She pulls Deena away from the curb, and swings Deena's hand in hers, back and forth. "Let's dance," she says.

They move around to the music from the radio, over the dried patches of oil on the the asphalt. Deena's mother tries to twirl around, but of course Deena is too small to hold her mother's hand while her mother spins under it, so she has to let go. Her mother steps away, then turns back and scoops Deena into her arms, and they are both spinning, the road and the horses and the gas pumps and the old truck blurring together until Deena feels suddenly nauseated.

"Put me down please, Mommy," she says. "I feel sick."

Her mother stops abruptly and sets her down. The world still revolves crazily; Deena takes a step and staggers, then stands still waiting for it to stop.

"I just wanted to dance," her mother says. She looks sad and defeated, staring off across the road. "Drink your Coke," she says. "I'll go see if there's something to eat inside." She turns and walks into the garage.

Deena has a method of drinking soda that involves punching a tiny hole in the pop top with a safety pin, so you can't tell the can has even been opened, then shaking it up and holding it away from her so that a thin pressurized stream shoots into her mouth. At home she liked to leave the empties in the refrigerator, so her mother would think there was soda when there wasn't, and would reach for one when she was thirsty and find nothing.

Deena can't find a safety pin in the gas station office, but she sees a thumbtack holding a postcard to the wall and pries it out to use it. The postcard shows a weathervane with a winged iron horse on top. The horse's front hooves are raised in the air, its tail streaming out behind it. She carefully puts the thumbtack back through the hole in the card and into its spot on the wall, and goes outside to sit on the curb.

She closes her eyes and tilts her head back, drinking. She hears her mother's heels clicking back and forth on the garage floor, hears her laugh.

"I bet you look awful good when you clean up," her mother says. "How do you get that grease off you, anyway?"

The mechanic mumbles something Deena can't quite hear, but it makes her mother laugh again.

"Oh, really," her mother says. "I bet you say that to all the damsels in distress."

"Only the pretty ones," the mechanic says.

"You keep any beer back here?" her mother says.

Deena stands and walks over to where her mother's lighter fell. She picks it up and walks around to the other side of the pumps, where the nozzles are.

"Got some beer in that cooler down there," the mechanic says. "Probably not yet chilled, though."

Deena unhooks a nozzle from the pump, struggling to lift it up and out of its cradle. She lays it down on the asphalt and squats before it. A little gas drips out; she sticks her finger in the puddle, no bigger than a nickel, and brings it up to her nose. She flicks the lighter and imagines a sheet of flame rising between her and her mother, a fiery wall; she sees her mother trying to get to her, then giving up finally and backing away from the heat, the hair along her arms singed and crackling, while Deena rises into the sky and flies away.

She tries the lighter several times, but it still won't work. She peers between the pumps at her mother, standing in the dim garage. Her mother holds a cigarette in her right hand and cradles her elbow in the other as she brings the cigarette to her red lips. She takes a drag, blows out smoke and flicks the ash to the floor.

Deena wonders what town they are near now. No cars come down the road. The horses in the field have moved away from the fence, and are standing motionless at the far end. It's quiet except for her mother's voice, and the man's, and the radio announcer babbling behind them. Deena sweats inside her pajamas, feeling the heat rise into her like something coming up out of the ground. She squirts more Coke into her mouth and holds it there, feeling it get warmer and flatter; she holds it as long as she can, and then swallows it.

# scores

Loren tries to explain to me why baseball is different from other sports. He works as a shingler and sometimes as an artist's model, and when he is not working he paints and watches TV, especially baseball. In the six months we have been living together he has tried to interest me in the game, but I can't seem to get it.

Listen, Fran. It's the only game where the losing team can be trailing by a huge score, even, say, in the eighth inning, and still win. Now, suppose you've got a football game and one team is ahead 28-3 in the fourth quarter—

I try to suppose it, but my mind wanders. I am not very good with numbers, with scores and statistics. I lie back on the loft bed and stare at the ceiling, thinking about Sasha. Sasha is living in my old apartment. From the deck of this apartment, two blocks up the hill, I can see the green curtains I hung in the living room. Sometimes the window is open and I listen for Sasha playing the piano, and sometimes I think I hear him.

Fran. You're not listening.

Yes, I am. The baseball team can win, even if it's been losing.

Right. You see, baseball is *subtle*. It's not just bodies banging together—

I think of me and Sasha on my old bed, the pillows pushed to the floor and my head hanging over the edge, upside-down. I close my eyes to remember just how it felt. That was two days ago, and I won't see him for at least another week because he's gone to hear one of his pieces played by an orchestra somewhere in Tennessee.

Loren has stopped talking. He's sitting back against the wall, naked, a blue pillow in his lap. He takes a joint from the ledge under the window and lights it.

Honey, he says. You're a million miles away.

No, I'm not, I say. I take the pillow away and nuzzle my face into him. He puts Pierre Cardin powder in his underwear every morning and I like the smell. Loren puts his hand on my hair while I suck him. He doesn't make a sound. It used to bother me sometimes, but now it seems perfectly natural to make love with him in silence. Sasha likes to talk about what we are doing while we are doing it. When Loren wants me to stop sucking him he doesn't say anything, only pushes me away and reaches for a condom from the window ledge. I raise my head and look out the window, but I can't see my old apartment from here. All I can see is the sky, and constellations whose names I learned once and forgot. When I close my eyes they are still there, like sunspots. Loren gently turns me onto my back and guides himself in.

I have a job now, doing marketing research. I call people on the phone and ask their opinions of district elections, carbonated soft drinks, health care plans for

those over forty-five. Often the people hang up on me,
but sometimes they are friendly and cooperative. After
we finish with the survey they will stay on the phone
and talk to me. I have made a friend this way, a woman
named Nicky. Sometimes when I'm tired of people hanging up on me I will call her number just to talk, though
when the supervisor walks by I have to pretend to be
interviewing her. I put on a formal tone and say, What
brand of cereal do you buy most often?

Nicky is married to an Army officer. She lives at The
Presidio with him and their two boys, and she goes to an
Army psychiatrist because her husband hits her and
screams at the boys. If there is a war her husband is supposed to interrogate any prisoners that are taken. She
talks to me about how she wants to leave him. I felt close
to Nicky immediately, in a way that I do not feel with
other women I meet. Nicky is as afraid of things as I am,
so maybe that is why I feel drawn to her. She feels like
my best friend, and I talk to her often inside my head,
about how I feel scared to leave Loren because he takes
care of me and helps me. I am doing much better than
before I lived with him; I go out to stores, I work, I stare
at the uniformed men on the TV screen and try to make
some sense, some order, out of how they throw and hit
the ball. But really I don't get it, and my head aches, and
I think they are just covering up the fact that the TV is
nothing but a tangle of tubes and wires underneath the
screen.

I work from four to nine p.m. weekdays. I am paid
cash, forty dollars each day. I often spend it right away,
before going home. I come home with liters of Pepsi or
orange gladiolas from the all-night stand or bags of giant pretzels from the vendor. Or I go to Walgreen's, where
I buy makeup and colored markers and a little dog with
batteries that barks when I push a button. I think it is a
cocker spaniel, and I have decided it is a girl. Here, girl, I
say, setting her up on the kitchen floor and moving away,
holding the leash. Loren scowls at me. He doesn't like

me to spend all my money on the way home, on things we don't need.

Buy toilet paper once in a while, he says. Buy milk, get some Comet, for Christ's sake. The bathroom is filthy.

He heats a can of chili and leaves some in the pan for me, then goes into the dining room and turns on the TV. I push the button, and the little dog starts toward me.

Sasha is back, but he hasn't called. In the afternoons on my way to work I walk slowly past my old apartment, looking up to the third floor. I know he is sitting in there at his Baldwin baby grand, or at the little slanted table where he copies scores for other composers. When Sasha is composing he sits cross-legged on the piano bench, naked or wearing nothing but a T-shirt, his shoulders hunched. Afterwards he does yoga, or runs, and then takes a hot bath. Sasha lives a very structured life. Within structure lies true freedom, he says. I sit on the front steps for a while but he doesn't come out, so I go to work.

I walk all the way there, down Market Street past the clothing stores and restaurants, past the porno theaters and the street people and a girl who tries to sell me incense. Hare Krishna, she says. She smiles at me, and I tell her maybe I will buy some later, after work. I never take the bus to work because I don't like being closed in with a lot of people under those lights. Also, when a bus passes me at night all lit up I see the faces of the people in it very clearly, and I don't want anyone looking in on me like that. I am careful to walk down the middle of the sidewalk, away from doorways and alleys, away from the curb where someone could pull up and open a car door. I try to keep my face blank, my step purposeful. I turn up California Street and walk two more blocks and take the elevator to the fourteenth floor. I fix myself a cup of coffee before sitting down at my station.

Tonight we are supposed to call people and offer them a free teeth-cleaning from a qualified hygienist. I try to call Nicky, but her husband answers so I only ask him if he would like me to schedule him for a dental examination. I can hear a child crying in the background, and dishes banging.

No, thank you, he says, very politely. I am in the Army; we have our own dentists.

Thank you for your time, I say. I hang up and call Sasha.

How often do you have your teeth cleaned? Would you be interested in a comprehensive dental examination at a very low cost?

Fran.

This is a professional call, I say.

Look, I've been swamped since I got back. And I can't just call you anytime. What if Loren answers the phone?

I know.

Look, Fran, I don't feel too good about this. I mean, now that you're living with Loren. You need some stability.

I need you, Sasha. I miss you. I think about you when I'm in bed with Loren. But I never think about Loren when I'm in bed with you. Don't you want to be with me anymore?

It's disruptive, Sasha says. I have a lot of work to do right now.

So do I. I have a lot of calls to make right now.

Frannie. Don't be mad.

I am not mad, I say. I just hate you. I hate your music. It doesn't even sound like music. I can't hum anything you write. Why don't you write something I can hum, Sasha? Why don't you want to see me? I always do what you want. I let you fuck me in the ass. I let you—

Calm down. Look, we'll get together and talk soon, okay? Okay? Don't get upset. Don't do anything crazy. We'll talk.

I'm not crazy.

I didn't say you were crazy. Look, Fran, I have to finish copying out some parts.

I'm not crazy. I have a job. I have a friend. I buy things. I could buy you some music paper.

I have to go. Call me tomorrow and we'll talk about it.

When my shift is over I wash out my coffee cup in the sink at the back of the office, then dry it and put it in my purse. I always take my cup home, so no one else will use it. I walk back along Market Street, looking for the girl with the incense, but she isn't around anymore.

At home Loren is painting in front of the TV. Loren's paintings disturb me and I don't like to look at them, so I sit down and watch the TV.

There's some stir-fry on the stove for you, Loren says.

Thank you, I say.

Sasha just called, he says, coming over to sit next to me on the couch.

Oh.

Is that all you have to say? You want to know what we talked about?

I don't care.

Sasha told me, Loren says.

Told you what?

Christ, Fran, don't pull this shit. I know you've been seeing each other.

I don't say anything. I draw up my feet onto the couch and put my head between my knees. Maybe this time Loren will hit me; he has almost hit me twice before, but each time he has stopped himself. It is very hard to stop yourself from doing something when you are angry, or when you want to do it very badly. I understand this, someone explained it to me, someone who could not help himself. He would sometimes cry afterwards and say he was sorry. He might even stop for a week or two, but then I would look up from doing my homework at the dining room table, and he would be sitting on the couch in front of the TV, next to my mother, but watching me.

I wait, hugging my knees, singing softly inside my head over and over, the way I used to. I hear Loren sigh and get up from the couch.

This isn't working, Fran, he says.

I don't move or think, I just try to concentrate on the music in my head. But I keep hearing Sasha's music, a lot of fast notes and then silence, and then a few notes all jumbled together. I let out a sound, but it's not loud enough to stop the notes so I rock back and forth and hold my ears and scream. It feels good to scream. Loren starts shaking me by the shoulders and saying my name over and over. I hear it like one steady note under all the others, *Fran Fran Fran* bong bong bong. Finally it's louder and drowns out everything else. Loren holds me.

Don't leave me, I say.

Shhh, Loren says. It's all right now.

Nicky writes poetry. She recites it to me on the phone, and I tell her how beautiful it is. The poems are romantic, full of flowers and sunsets. People walk hand in hand along the beach, stopping to pick up shells. Pigeons fly up from plazas and turn gold in the sun.

I'm leaving him, Nicky says. I can't talk long, she says. He'll be home any minute and I've barely started dinner.

Where will you go? Do you have any money?

I have to get a job first. Then I can save for an apartment.

Maybe we can get an apartment together, I say. I can save, too.

Oh, let's do that! Nicky says.

I want a garden, I say. I have never had a garden. I could grow things for us to eat. Tomatoes, for example. And artichokes.

Carrots, Nicky says, and onions and broccoli and lettuce. We can make big salads, we won't spend anything on food, and we'll be thin, too.

I'm already thin, I tell her. Loren says I should remember to eat, but sometimes food is the furthest thing from my mind.

I should lose a few pounds, Nicky says. He calls me a pig, she says. He calls me a fat pig even when we make love. If he catches me eating anything sweet he hits me. I feel so ugly. I'm depressed all the time and then I eat because I'm depressed. It's a vicious circle.

I'm sure you're not ugly. You write beautiful poems.

I want to kill him sometimes, Nicky says. I just want to take one of his guns and shoot him dead. I have to go, she says. Talk to you tomorrow?

I'll try. There is a different supervisor tomorrow; he watches everyone constantly.

I make a few calls to find out what kind of hair products people use. Shampoo? Creme rinse? Styling gel or spray? Do you color your hair yourself or go to a salon? One man says, Hey, I'm a bald guy. He laughs and asks me what color hair I have.

Pale blonde, I say.

How about your eyes?

Blue, like cornflowers.

You must be a knockout, he says. Want to go out sometime?

No, thank you, I say.

Too bad, he says. Chance of a lifetime.

I have a boyfriend. He takes care of me. I'm afraid of things, and he helps me.

Well, the man says. Nothing to be afraid of. Come on, he says. We won't tell your boyfriend.

I have a confession to make, I say. I really have brown hair and eyes. When Nicky leaves her husband we're going to move in together and have a garden and be safe from everything.

Who's Nicky? She your girlfriend?

My best friend.

Well, bring her along, the man says. We'll have a party. What time do you get off?

Nine o'clock.

I'll bet you work downtown in one of those big office buildings.

Yes. How did you know that?

Psychic, the man says. Come on, how about it? Take a chance. Let me buy you a friendly drink.

I think to myself, I don't want to take any chances. I have to be careful. Then I think of how Sasha won't see me anymore, and how Loren is probably going to leave me. I think about my stepfather, how he never covered my mouth with his hand, how I could have screamed anytime but didn't. I think of the other man, the one last year. I remember lying behind the dumpster while he grunted above me. I didn't make a sound. I tried not to even breathe.

I tell him I will meet him at a bar on Market Street, one I pass every night on the way home. I've always wanted to go in, but I've been too afraid to push open the padded doors with their round windows to see what is inside, in the darkness. I tell him to meet me in front of the bar, so I will not have to go in alone, and he says he'll be there.


A man stands in front of home plate, tugging at the brim of his cap. He swings the bat a few times, practicing. When the pitcher throws the ball he swings again, and misses.

Three and two, the man says. Top of the ninth. You like baseball?

Not really, I say. But I watch the TV above the bar to see what happens next. The man orders us more drinks. He's not nervous about asking the bartender if she has a certain kind of whisky. On the TV, the player watches the next ball go by him. He almost swings but then stops. He drops the bat and walks away.

Was that a ball or a strike, I say. I feel a little drunk, and wonder if I will be able to walk home.

Strike, the man says. He puts his hand on my hair and strokes it. I pick up my drink, sipping it, not looking at him. I watch the screen, the big green field where men in white uniforms are spread out like a handful of stars, connected toeach other in a pattern I can't figure out. The man puts his arm around me.

You're a good-looking girl, he says. He squeezes my shoulders, and then his face is close to mine. He pushes his lips against me. He sticks his tongue in my mouth before I can clench my teeth to stop him.

You taste good too, he says. He squeezes my shoulders again, and his other hand falls heavily into my lap. I take another sip of my drink and stare at the TV, but I'm not seeing it anymore. It's nothing but a black box, with coils of intestines writhing around like snakes. It looks like one of Loren's paintings, which are dark and full of strange shapes that almost look like recognizable parts of bodies.

The man 's hand moves to my crotch, and I close my eyes. I imagine me and Nicky in a pretty garden, standing among vines of plump tomatoes. I can smell them, ripe and seedy, and feel how hot it is standing there in the sun. Little insects whiz around us. Golden birds are singing in the trees, a hummingbird hovers among the flowers. I want to stay there forever and never come back, but someone is saying Stop it, stop it, and I have to open my eyes; I have to look right at him and tell him to leave me alone.

# the chair

He could hear every move they made; their floor—his ceiling—was so thin. If he'd had a gun he could have shot their toes off anytime. Right now he could hear her rocking back on two legs of a kitchen chair, the man shuffling to the refrigerator in slippers. She thumped the front two legs down hard. He gritted his teeth. He hated living in this building, hated the beeping of trucks backing up outside his window all day and in the middle of the night, but he could not afford to move. His wife had kicked him out, and he was on Unemployment. He waited for his neighbors to go to bed, and for a few hours it was quiet, but at three in the morning they started making it. The bed scraped back and forth monotonously on the floorboards. It sounded like some animal was patiently digging a hole into his apartment. His wife had fallen in love with someone else and now they were man and wife and he was nothing, an insect about to be devoured by an enormous anteater that any minute now would poke its long proboscis through and vacuum him into oblivion. He leaped out of bed and grabbed an antique chair he had once bought for his wife who said she loved it until she decided to redecorate her life; he raised the chair above his head and pounded the ceiling with it. "Stop it!" he screamed. *WHAM WHAM. WHAM.* The legs went through the ceiling. Surprised, he let go. A little white powder shook loose and fell in his face. Above him, two more tentative scrapes. Then silence. He could hear his breathing, loud and ragged. The chair hung there, upside down. He started laughing and couldn't stop, even when they pounded a shoe and the chair fell and broke to pieces on the floor.

# reading sontag

He's a submissive. She's used to giving men what they want. At first she doesn't know this about him; they dance in a living room, end up in a bedroom, he leans back against the wall while she kisses him. She presses her palms against his, and he sags against the wall, the backs of his hands touching it. She's much smaller than he is. She doesn't know how to be dominant, but she wants to please him.

A piece of pornographic fiction concocts no better than a crude excuse for a beginning; and once having begun, it goes on and on and ends nowhere.

The next time, when they start to fuck, he lies back on the bed with his arms over his head. The next time it's a few nights later, or the next morning. There is no next time. Even if there is, there won't be many more. This is my way of recovering the past, in order to torment my-self with it. The next time, he lies back on the bed, tells her to use his dick for her pleasure. She uses his dick for her pleasure. She doesn't come. She comes. She almost comes, stays at an excruciating peak for what feels like hours, shuffles through erotic images and fantasies try-ing to break through. No, trying to let go. Surrender? No, break through is better. It's a barrier. A wall. Or maybe glass. Trying to break through a barrier that feels like glass. Trying to forget someone else. She's a little girl. He's a priest, he makes her kneel beside a narrow bed in the rectory, he pulls her dress over her head but not off, he takes off her underwear and fucks her. She's a nun. He rips off her rosary. She's in a bathroom, one of a row of naked women on their knees, men come in to fuck them, then go to take a piss. He's pissing in her mouth. Literature's supposed to take the moral high ground. To be beautiful. To instruct. To cast out one's personal de-mons. To revel in one's neurotic self-obsession.

It's so difficult to make love with someone new—much harder than it used to be, when she was younger. She's been celibate for years. Okay, months. It feels like months, anyway. She remembers making love with her ex-hus-band. Bastard. Asshole. Love of her life. She hates him. She misses him constantly, constantly feels the pain of their failure, or the pain of her failure, the pain of his abandonment, the pain of the loss of their intense sexual pleasure, pain, pain, pain. She starts to cry. She doesn't let herself cry. They stop fucking, and he runs her a bath and leaves her alone. She curls up in the tub, lifts hand-fuls of white soapsuds, lets them drop onto her breasts in the candlelight. She's in a fetal position. An image of extreme distress. Duress. Inability to cope. Whatever. The obsessions of *Histoire de l'Oeil* are indeed Bataille's own. In other words, there's supposed to be a gap. A disclaimer. A lie. Okay, a disclaimer. The conditions of my grant were that I not write anything obscene. I signed the paper. I lied to get food stamps, to stay on MediCal, and to receive Unemployment. I also signed the Drug Free Workplace Enforcement Act. I have never used drugs in my life. She stays in the tub until the water gets almost cold, then goes back to the bedroom. They light up a joint. They snort some coke, shoot some heroin, and smoke some crack, then another couple—friends of his—shows up, and the four of them fuck in every conceivable combination. Lots of homoerotic activity: the men come in each other's mouth, stick crucifixes up each other's ass. The women put their tongues all over each other. She likes fucking his male friend; the friend dominates her, the way she's used to. About four in the morning she and the friend end up in the shower together, masturbating for each other, and she asks for his number. He asks to see her again. He asks if he can call her. She refuses. She hesitates. She doesn't know what she says, she's so disoriented from all the drugs. She's pyschically dislocated. They gave me a lot of money; it didn't once occur to me to refuse it. Maybe I should have turned it down, to gain some notoriety. I'm a nobody. No one cares if I live or die.

A few days later they're discussing another couple, mutual friends.

Why do things always have to go somewhere? he says.

Now she has to take the opposite role, though she might, herself, have asked the same question. She feels a sense of panic that they won't go anywhere; he'll resist her, or be indifferent. She's afraid to show weakness around him. When they make love, when they fuck, when they perform for each other, for you, for us, when they engage in perversely pleasurable sexual activity, when they begin to have mutual boundary problems, when they fuck, she thinks about slapping his face, remembering the lover who slapped her. Remembering her ex-husband, the failure, etc., on and on, she must be addicted to pain. I, for one, am sick of her. She's history.

He knows she's used to giving men what they want. He's prepared to be disappointed in her. His own heart's still broken from the last affair, which, though brief, was intense. He's still hurting from the last relationship, which, though intense, was brief. Experiences aren't pornographic; only images and representations—structures of the imagination—are. This I underlined and felt compelled to write a note in the margin: "But if 'experience' exists in our consciousness/imagination of it.. ?" I think I was trying to say that what we experience, as it's partly a function of how we perceive, can't be abstracted, separated from structures of imagination. But now, when I think about it, I'm not sure. I'm not intellectually equipped to take on Susan Sontag. I'm stupid. No, I'm smart, but I lack depth and breadth of knowledge. I skim everything in a desperate attempt to catch up. I'll never catch up. Normally we don't experience, at least don't want to experience, our sexual fulfillment as distinct from or opposed to our personal fulfillment. But perhaps in part they are distinct, whether we like it or not. She wrote this in 1967. Nothing's changed. Some things have changed. Not enough has changed. No one will publish my work; I'm a terrible writer; I can't write a conventional, realistic story. I've given up. Still, I keep trying. He's prepared to be disappointed in her, but she keeps surprising him. Their sex gets better and better. He wants to hold on to his pain, his heartbreak, his regret, but that position begins to feel unnatural; he realizes he's only trying to deepen the loss of the other relationship to satisfy some twisted need to see himself as a victim, to re-create his childhood abandonment. If only he could see this, he might love her, but he holds on to his pain and finally breaks off the relationship. Affair. Friendship. Their random couplings. Meaningless sexual interludes. Temporary evasions of the acute meaninglessness of existence.

They go to a bar. Bataille hunches at a table in the corner, scribbling in a notebook. Marie is sprawled in a chair, naked, her legs open, being sucked by Pierot. They order beers. No, gin. He orders Johnny Walker Red, she has a rum and Coke. They stand at the bar, fascinated by the scene. Arousal comes through identification with one of the participants. In fantasies, she often sees herself from the male point of view. Not the dark beneath the blindfold, the feel of the black cloth knotted behind her head, but the sight of her face, her mouth open as he fucks her there. Marie climbs up on the table and squats, pissing on the dwarf. He decides to take a picture of the dwarf, urine splashing in his face, being jerked off by Pierot. He manages to get part of his own face in the shot by pointing the camera at the mirror behind the bar. Later, in his darkroom, he processes the negative, hits it with the enlarger light, moves the paper around in the developing bath with a pair of gray plastic tongs. The bottles behind the bar, the mirror, Marie's white body, the stream of urine. Where his face should be, the paper stays blank. Fuck him, I'm going to forget all about him.

He doesn't believe in Plato's concept of men and women as halves of the same whole, seeking each other. He's been through Reichean therapy. He's been depressed. He's fine alone. He's bald as an egg; she imagines straddling him, pushing her cunt against his mouth, then sliding it across his skull. His head is nicely shaped; she can't imagine spoiling its purity with hair. He takes her nipple gently in his teeth and gives it a slight tug. Milk pours out of it, thin and watery and sweet, filling his mouth almost faster than he can swallow. He sucks and sucks, feels drunk, falls asleep in her arms. She gets up, carries him to his crib, loosens the suction between them. She tucks the covers around him, spins the colored plastic mobile that hangs from the ceiling, touches the pulsing spot on his translucent forehead. She feels incomplete without a lover in her life, realizes that after years of dodging commitment—entrapment—commitment—she wants a partner. A companion. Anyone who will hold her and love her. A male body in her bed. A confirmation that she exists. When she doesn't see him for several days, the intimacy she'd felt with him earlier vanishes as though it never existed. Each time they're together, it feels as though they're beginning over.

He can't guess what she's thinking; when he asks, she says, *It's private,* sounding almost angry. He's beginning to resent the relationship. Affair. Etc. She can make him do anything she wants. He feels trapped. Manipulated. Toyed with. He's tired of living without much of a context, or one that shifts so radically. Maybe he's going insane. He's stopped taking Prozac, stopped therapy, stopped calling her. He's tired of having to fuck her all the time. He loves fucking her; he can't get enough. He goes through all his photographs of old lovers, but they're like movie stills of famous actors; familiar as they are, he knows he's never met them. He lights a cigarette from the pack that appears on the table. His dick throbs in his jeans. He's going to explode unless he fucks her. He unzips his jeans and jerks off. There's no difference between inner and outer life. He comes thinking of her, milk pouring from his dick, come pouring from his dick like milk, like wine, like a language he'll never learn.

# emergency room

He asks if I've been tied up before. I tell him yes, and he wants to know for how long. Tell me about it, he says. I feel shy, I don't want to go into details. We're sitting in Vesuvio's at four in the afternoon, drinking gin and tonics. He has his hand on my thigh. I'm madly in love with him; we've known each other three weeks. I'm not ambivalent like I usually am; everything about him seems perfect: his close-cut black hair, the way he puts his tongue down my throat when he kisses me, his blunt, square hands. He's the sexiest man I've ever been with. It scares me I can feel so happy. None of our friends think it will last.

I want to tie you up, he says. I want to do things with you that you've never done with anyone.

A man at the bar is doing card tricks. He holds up the queen of diamonds and shows it to a pale, pretty girl in a black leather minidress, black fishnet tights and heavy black combat boots. The girl looks bored. She glances over at us and sees me watching her. She takes a card from the magician's deck, looks at it and sticks it back in.

We get drunk sitting in Vesuvio's. At seven o'clock we're still there, kissing passionately, his hand under my T-shirt squeezing my breast. No one pays any attention to us. The magician is still there, too, talking to another woman. He holds up the queen of hearts. Finally we get hungry and walk around the corner to Brandy Ho's and eat Kung Pao chicken and Szechuan shrimp, sitting next to each other in the red leather booth. I feel like I'm in an alternate universe. Everything looks familiar but it's different than before. The sexual intoxication is overwhelming; I can't function in the real world: I haven't called my friends, paid my bills, read a newspaper since all this started. I don't want it ever to end. I feel vulnerable and it's terrifying; I can't help being in love with him, even if he leaves me or treats me like shit, I can't hold back the way I usually do, I have to give him everything. Then I won't know who I am anymore.


With his glasses on he looks like a different person: shy, slightly studious, younger. It's like he's in disguise; I don't recognize him as the same person I fuck. I like him in his glasses, like the idea that there are things about him no one could ever guess from the way he looks. He takes his glasses off, sets them on my kitchen table.

Take off your clothes and stand against the wall, he says.

I peel off my T-shirt, drop my skirt and underwear, and lean against the wall, facing him. He tells me to put my arms above my head. We've just finished dinner. He pours himself more wine and tips his chair back, drinking the wine, watching me.

Don't move, he says. He leaves the kitchen. I hear him pissing in the bathroom. I'm excited, scared I don't know what's going to happen next. I close my eyes, listen to the stream of piss hitting the water in the bowl. My neighbor in the next apartment starts playing the clarinet. She's just learning so it's all honks and squeaks. The walls are thin, I'm worried someone will hear us, I don't want anyone to hear us. I don't want anyone to know what we do together, what he does to me.

He comes back to the kitchen, zipping his pants. He takes an apple from the bowl of fruit on the table.

Open your mouth.

He shoves the apple against my mouth; my teeth sink into it. I'm gagged. He's not gagging me. I can drop the apple anytime. I want him to dominate me, use me; I want to be his slave. I have to understand submission, why it's so erotic for me; I can't reconcile it with the rest of my life. I've never let myself physically explore how I feel because intellectually I can't accept it. Women are shit, they're only here for men's pleasure, men control everything.

My beautiful slut, he says. Look how wet you are. He puts his middle finger inside me, then in his mouth. He unbuckles his belt and takes it off in one smooth motion.


One Saturday night when we're fucking, the condom breaks. I know I'm ovulating, I don't want to get pregnant. He calls a sex information hotline and asks what we can do, and they tell him there's an abortion pill I can take; I should call a doctor to prescribe it.

I call the advice line at Kaiser and get put on hold. I wait forty-five minutes, then a voice comes on the line and says there's one more call ahead of me. I wait ten more minutes. The woman on the other end tells me she can't help me, I need to talk to Doctor X. I ask her to connect me. She connects me to the wrong extension; the people there tell me to call a different number. I hang up, dial the main hospital and ask for Doctor X.

He's not on tonight.

I explain what's happening. The woman on the other end insists that Doctor X isn't there, and no one else can prescribe the pill. Finally someone else gets on the phone and tells me that Doctor X is being paged. I'm put on hold again. A muzak version of "Light My Fire" plays, followed by the Beatles' "Here, There and Everywhere." Twenty minutes later another person gets on the line.

Can I help you?

I think I'm being helped. I don't know. I've been on the phone for an hour and a half, I'm trying to reach Doctor X.

I want to scream at the person on the phone, but she is very nice, it's not her fault, there's nobody to blame, I don't want to scream at her. I don't want to have a baby. I'm thirty years old, I work at a cafe and never have enough money for art materials. My mother was a painter; she stopped after she had me. I can't be a painter if I have a baby. He doesn't want a baby either. Not this way, he says. Not by accident.

Please hold, the nice person says. I listen to a few bars of "My Cherie Amor." A minute later Doctor X gets on the line.

You have to come to the Emergency Room to pick it up, he says.

Can't you just call it in to a drugstore?

We have to see you, he says. There are certain risks involved.

He says that if the pills don't work and the fetus is female it could be turned into a boy by the hormones. Masculinized, he says. The fetus might be masculinized, and if you decide to have the baby there could be problems.

I don't want to have the baby, I say. I want the pills. If they don't work I'll have an abortion. Please, I say. Can't you call it in?

You have to come to the Emergency Room, he repeats, sounding annoyed. We have to have a record that we've seen you.

76

I hang up. It's ten p.m.; we haven't had any dinner. He puts his arms around me.

He says, I hate to see you go through this.

I hate doctors, I say. I hate western medicine. I hate Kaiser, you never see the same doctor twice. Nobody knows you or gives a shit about you, you're a name on a chart. Why can't they just give me the pills?

Let's go eat first, he says. I'll take you someplace nice, we'll forget about this bullshit. The Emergency Room will be open all night.


He takes me to Little Italy. We drink a lot of wine. I start to feel better, now it's an adventure we're having together instead of a lousy experience. We joke about it, he puts his hand over mine on the red-and-white checkered tablecloth. I've never been so in love with anyone. I tell him I don't think I want any children.

I'll get sterilized, I say. I'll make an appointment and get my tube tied. I only have one tube and ovary because I had an infection once and had to have an operation. A gynecologist told me once that if I ever got sterilized it might be major surgery because of the scar tissue from the other operation.

I'll get a vasectomy, he says. It's easier, it's just an office procedure.

What if we break up and you want to have a baby with someone else? As I say this the thought of it makes me jealous and depressed, and I'm sure it will happen.

I can go to a sperm bank, then. Besides we're not going to break up. And you might change your mind. Five years from now we might want a baby, and we could have one.

We get to the Emergency Room a little before midnight. We sit in the waiting room, and after about half an hour a nurse leads me through a curtain and takes my blood pressure.

I'm only here to pick up a prescription, I tell her.

She ignores me, fastens a yellow plastic ID bracelet with my name and policy number around my wrist. She leads me to an examining room where there's a metal table with stirrups, and lays a blue plastic gown on the table.

Wait here, she says.

I sit down on the only chair. After forty-five minutes a Chinese medical student comes in.

I need to examine you, he says.

No, you don't. I'm not sick, I just need a prescription.

I'm supposed to examine you.

I think of him looking at me, my legs spread apart, my heels in the cold stirrups; I don't want him to look at me. I start crying and saying I just want the pills, there's nothing wrong with me, I don't want a baby you don't need to examine me, please just give me the pills so I can go home.

He writes something down on his chart, then walks out, muttering something I can't hear. A minute later the nurse says I can go back to the waiting room.

A man with long blond hair is passed out in one of the chairs. Three well-dressed black people are sitting together. The man is doubled over, holding his side, and the two women are on either side of him talking to him and rubbing his shoulders. There's a Toyota commercial on the TV, then an episode of "Miami Vice." The nurse comes out after twenty minutes and tells me that Kaiser's pharmacy doesn't have any more of the pills; there might be some at Mount Zion, she has to call and then send someone there to pick them up.

I lean my head on his shoulder; he strokes my hair. The blond man wakes up and looks around the room. Fuck this shit, he says. He gets up and walks out.

At three a.m. the nurse calls me in behind the curtain and hands me a paper cup of water and another paper cup with three tiny white pills in it. She gives me three more to take in twelve hours.

When we leave, the black people are still sitting there.

I have an almost pathological need for other people's approval. If someone criticizes me I fall apart, I feel useless, stupid, insignificant. When I confess this to him he says I need to learn not to internalize other people's negativity. I experience this as a subtle criticism and move to the edge of the bed, away from him.

I used to sleep with men so they would like me. I always had a lot of lovers. Now I only fuck him; he excites me more than anyone. When I masturbate I don't think about strangers fucking me, the way I used to; I think about him looping a rope through a ring screwed into the top of the doorframe, slapping my breasts and cunt. I think about the way he growls low in his throat, the violence of his orgasms. I masturbate imagining he is watching me, and come saying his name over and over. My life before I knew him seems impoverished, a desert. I'm afraid of losing him; he has to keep reassuring me that he loves me and wants me. At parties I'm jealous if he talks with other women. I'm convinced they're more attractive, more desirable than I am.

We're in someone's loft studio; it's too crowded. I feel like I'm suffocating. Everyone is talking to everyone else, huge paintings hang on the walls, the paint laid on layer after layer—thick dark colors, blues and blacks. I can't find him. No one is talking to me. Someone gave me some mushrooms earlier and now I'm starting to come on to them; I feel jumpy and want to find something to drink to calm me down. I bump into a woman, she stares at me in dislike, turns away. I get through the crowd and pour myself some wine, drink it quickly and pour another one, asking people if they've seen him. No one has. I'm panicked, sure he's met another woman and left with her.

I go into the bathroom and lock the door. I feel sick so I crouch at the toilet but I can't throw up. Sitting down on the floor, my back against the wall, I stare at the postcards tacked above the toilet. I know I'm seeing images but I can't tell my brain what they are, specifically; they're like abstract paintings, they have no meaning. I feel violated by images, I can't help seeing them on billboards, TV, in ads and movies; they get into me through osmosis and change my thought patterns: what I'm supposed to look like, feel like, be. I close my eyes and see blue snowflakes.

He's pounding on the door, his voice sounds far away. I get up and open it. He takes me in his arms.

Please fuck me, I say. Fuck me here, on the floor.

He locks the door and undresses me. I lie down on the floor; it's cold, I start shivering. He takes off his shirt and tucks it under me. He's standing over me, unzipping his black leather pants. I start hallucinating that he's a demon, his eyes are frightening—dark brown, he's wearing his contacts so there's a yellowish ring around his irises. I realize I don't trust him, I'm afraid he'll hurt me. I want him to hurt me.

Slap me.

He slaps me across the face. I feel myself clench, get wet. My head lolls to the side; he looks in my eyes, I'm naked, I'm begging him to do it again. He takes a condom from his pants pocket and puts it on, then slaps me again and enters me. I start to come almost immediately.

Not yet, he says, and stops moving inside me.

Please, I say, thrusting up at him, I'll go crazy if I don't finish coming. He stays still while I writhe under him; the orgasm goes on and on, I can't seem to stop. After a while he starts fucking me again, faster and faster, he comes with a loud moan and falls all the way on top of me.

I feel secure again feeling his weight, listening to his heart slowing down.

I talk to my friend Simone on the phone; we haven't spoken for weeks. She tells me about her lover, whom she's just broken up with.

At first it was great, she says. We did things sexually we'd never done with anyone else. But then he confessed that he likes to cross-dress. I mean, I just couldn't handle it. He wanted me to pretend he had a cunt; it was too weird.

I don't talk about my sex life to Simone; at least, not the really intimate details. My girlfriends and I discuss the size of our lovers' cocks, tell each other if they're any good in bed; I told Simone about the time I met two guys in North Beach and went to the Holiday Inn with them. Simone likes being tied up, but I don't want to talk about it with her. He and I have our own private world, we spend hours together absorbed in each other, seeing how far we can go. We close the curtains, nothing gets in. I tell Simone I want to marry him.

You're kidding, Simone says. How long have you known this guy?

Ten weeks.

Forget it, Simone says.

No, I mean it. I've been with enough men. I don't want to do that anymore.

The Virtuous Woman, Simone says.

Something like that.

You can't do it. You know how you are—if you like somebody and he wants you, you let him fuck you.

But I never felt like this about anybody else. And he's the best lover I ever had, I know I couldn't find anybody else who does what he does for me.

It's not about better, Simone says. Sooner or later you'll want something different, something he can't give you, and you'll go out looking for it. And anyway, you're confusing sex with love. You're hot for this man so you think you love him.

I wonder why Simone does this to me; she can't be happy for me, she always finds flaws. He says she's just being my friend, trying to protect me. I don't call Simone for weeks because I'm afraid she'll convince me that she's right.

## *in the box called pleasure*

The more I fuck him, the more I want him; I've never had this much sex with anyone before. It's all we do— sex, work, eat, sleep. Sometimes we don't get around to cooking dinner until midnight, and sometimes we end up at two a.m. eating cheese and olives and pita bread in bed. Simone tells my other friends I'm obsessed. He's late for work all the time; his boss blames it on me. No one understands us. There's a conspiracy against us, to separate us. Romantic love is always tragic; the lovers can't stay together, death or lies or fate separate them. It's dangerous to be erotic, then you aren't so trapped; if you do it in public they look at you and their minds are filthy so they see filth, then they try to put you in jail.

After a few more weeks we quit our jobs and move to a hotel in the Tenderloin where we can be together all the time; between us we have enough money for about four months. I don't know what's going to happen after that and I don't care. I set up my tubes of paints, my chalks and charcoals and brushes, on a table in the corner of the room, and he models for me. We have a small refrigerator with a freezer that keeps tiny ice cubes frozen in plastic trays, a hot plate, an indoor barbecue, a stack of books we've bought over the years meaning to read but that we never got around to; we have a portable cassette player, tapes, potted violets and an aloe plant. We never go farther than the corner grocery half a block away. We cook or eat takeout Vietnamese food from next door. Whatever we need from the outside world, the son of the woman two doors down picks up for us. We fight sometimes. We fall more deeply in love. Underneath everything we're blissfully happy. We know how to live. All we want is for you to go away and leave us the fuck alone.

# 'til there was you

*Practice*

The band practices in the basement of the keyboard player's mother's house in San Jose. Every Wednesday, the mother's bowling night, the band members set up their amps and mikes and instruments in a tiny room whose walls are covered with carpet remnants from the warehouse where the lead guitarist works. The keyboard player's girlfriend watches TV in the mother's bedroom—"90210," then "Party of Five," then the news, or she restlessly surfs through the channels. She keeps the TV turned up loud to try and drown out the electric bass thumping up through the floor. The band members come upstairs to take a piss, to grab beers from the fridge, and roll joints from the baggie of pot on the kitchen table.

When the girlfriend goes into the kitchen, they say, Hey. How's it goin. She can tell they've forgotten her name. They are large men, in their thirties and forties—older than her and her boyfriend. She is twenty, and her boyfriend just turned twenty-two. The bass player has a long gray ponytail, the drummer has hair plugs, the lead guitarist remembers when Eric Clapton played with some band named Cream. They are losers, playing loser music that the lead singer, Tony, writes for them. The keyboard player's girlfriend hates Wednesday nights, but she always comes to practice, because she loves her boyfriend, and if he becomes a famous rock musician one day she will be able to say, I was with him from the beginning. Not that it's going to happen with this loser band, but the girlfriend keeps this opinion to herself. Her boyfriend is actually not that good on keyboards. At least, not yet. She is sure he'll improve, though. Tony says he has soul. Soul, like it's the fucking sixties. What a loser Tony is.

*Three Gigs*

1.
Tony gets them a gig in a local club. They play in the back room, a cavernous space with a balcony and black walls, where the stage is. In the front room, where the bar is, the place is packed. People at the bar are talking and laughing and putting dollars in the jukebox. In the back room there's no one but Tony's girlfriend, the keyboard player's girlfriend, and a drunk Texan in a white ten-gallon hat looking for the men's room. The band plays for an hour and a half, and between songs Tony talks to an imaginary crowd, saying things like, All right, people! Let's rock 'n roll! At one point he introduces each band member, and the two girlfriends clap. Tony says, Here's a song I wrote called "Downtown Streets." Feel free to get up and get down and *dance* to this one. Tony's girlfriend gets up and dances, alone in the center of the room.

84

The drunk Texan wobbles toward her like he's going to dance with her, but he runs into a chair on the way. His hat falls off. He bends down to pick it up, falls over, and decides to stay there. He takes off his jacket, folds it into a pillow, and curls up on the floor. Tony's girlfriend raises her arms in the air, twirling around, her hair flying. She has a degree in music from Curtis Institute in Philadelphia and plays weird experimental oboe in a different loser band. The keyboard player's girlfriend thinks, Well, there's someone for everyone. She goes off to the bar to get drunk.

2.

They play at a bar on Sixth Street in San Francisco—a neighborhood of junkies, crackheads, whores, alcoholics, and other people too poor or fucked up to be anywhere else. In the middle of the second set a fight breaks out between a man with a beer bottle and another man with a pool cue. Instead of going into the next song on the set list—a slow ballad called "Need to Need You"—Tony calls for "Starving" and starts singing at the top of his lungs: You just chew me up / and spit me out / like I'm rotten meat / well there's just no doubt / that you'll be starving for my lo-o-ove, babe / 'cause when push comes to sho-o-ove, babe. . . . That's as far as he gets before the man with the cue chases the man with the bottle onstage and into the drumset, knocking over the toms and cymbal stand. Everyone stops playing and watches the man wildly swinging his pool cue, narrowly missing the drummer. The man with the bottle runs into the street. Well, shit, the other man says, kicks over the snare and goes back to the pool table. By way of apology, the bar owner books them for another gig the following month. When they show up, the bar is gone and a Vietnamese restaurant is in its place. They lock their equipment in the bass player's van, sit down, and order dinner.

3.

They play at the Bay to Breakers, a race through the streets of San Francisco, at six a.m. on a Sunday morning. Thousands of runners stream past the outdoor stage. Tony shouts, sings, and stomps. He struts back and forth like an oversized Mick Jagger, a sleeveless black tank top riding up his beer belly, his bandanna headband soaked with sweat. San Francisco, I love you! he screams. Rock 'n roll forever! Runner after runner glances up at the stage and waves before pounding uphill and disappearing over the horizon. The keyboard player's girlfriend stands in front of the stage, one of the few stationary people, and even she is swept up in the excitement of the crowds and noise and color. Yeah! she cries after every song. She looks up at her boyfriend in his leather vest and torn jeans, standing at his KS-32 pounding out chord progressions, and thinks with pride: I have fucked him. I have tasted his cock in my mouth. A feeling of love and power surges through her. This is my future, she thinks; this is my fate.

*Personnel Changes*

The drummer quits after the bar fight. The band auditions a new guy, who happens to be blind. He hits his head going down the stairs to the basement. The friend who brought him refuses to leave the car; he sits in an old station wagon in the driveway, drinking beer and smoking cigarettes. The keyboard player's girlfriend walks into the kitchen and sees the friend through the window, his head thrown back, eyes closed, like he is listening to music on the radio. Good music, she thinks. Successful music. She can hear the new drummer trying to keep up while Tony sings, Never gonna die / never gonna give up. / Gonna make the world / fill my loving cup. She hears her boyfriend play a wrong chord, and then another one. In fact, he sounds like he's playing in a whole different key. By now she knows all Tony's songs by heart, and she can tell when somebody messes up.

A sense of hopelessness overtakes her, but as she listens to Tony sing she feels a promise in the words. I got my own vision / I got my own song. /Look out, world / 'cause it won't be long. Tony says they are going to cut a demo soon. He says a guy from a local cable-access TV show is going to come to the next gig. He says the band is going to play at the Great American Music Hall in San Francisco. Downstairs the music stops, and they start the song again. This time the drummer nails the beat, and her boyfriend gets most of the chords right. She closes her eyes, pretending she is blind, and stands in the kitchen listening until the song ends.

*Romance*

Tony's girlfriend gets pregnant, and they decide to get married. At the wedding, which is held on a ship that has been permanently docked and turned into a restaurant, Tony asks the hired band if he can do a number with them. Tony's band members, looking uncomfortable in suits and ties, sit holding plastic glasses of champagne while Tony sings an old Beatles song, "Til There Was You," to his new bride. Usually, Tony's band is so loud that Tony is practically drowned out. But today, for the first time, the keyboard player's girlfriend can hear his voice clearly, and she realizes that Tony can't sing very well. In fact, he has a tendency to sing a little flat. It's hard to tell if he notices; he stands holding the mike in both hands, gazing into his bride's eyes, while she weeps under her veil. The keyboard player is nowhere in sight. When his girlfriend goes to look for him she finds him in the coat room with one of the bridesmaids, his tongue in her mouth, his soulful hands slipped up under her shirt. The girlfriend screams at him, and in the next room, Tony hits the last high phrase of "Til There Was You," and his voice cracks.

*Where They Are Now*

One by one, everyone quit the band. The blind drummer played two gigs with them and disappeared; the old drummer came back for a while but then moved to Florida. The bass player got a job as Banquet Captain at the Ramada Inn by the airport and was too busy to be in a band anymore. The lead guitarist, who could actually play—he was the only reason they got any gigs at all—moved to LA and started doing session work. The keyboard player decided to quit music entirely because it was too fucking hard, and he hated practicing. Now he does computer graphics for a firm in Silicon Valley. Tony's wife had a girl; she's five now, and Tony, after a long break to cope with fatherhood and unemployment, is working in a music store and putting together a new band.

The keyboard player's girlfriend—now his ex-girlfriend—bought herself an electric bass guitar. She joined an all-female band named V. Dentata. Their debut album, *Hose Me Down*, has just gone platinum. Two of the singles from it—the title song and another one she herself wrote, "All F**ked Up and No Place to Go"—are on the Billboard Top Twenty. When she looks back on her time with the keyboard player, she can barely remember him. He's a pair of torn jeans, a Wednesday night TV schedule, a weak left hand. All she remembers with any clarity is Tony, her inspiration, the person who taught her everything important about the music.

# *but*

They'd known each other a month and had decided to marry, but two days before the wedding she hit him over the head with a beer bottle during an argument and the paramedics had to come and he got sixteen stitches but what the hell, they reconciled as soon as they were sober. And then the wedding, a party in the warehouse space he lived in, and everyone still drinking and dancing as they headed off to a big hotel in the city. But the friend who was going to loan them a Lincoln to arrive in style never showed up, so they took the groom's old car and pulled up and staggered into the lobby, but with his bandaged head and the two of them being pretty wasted and some kind of complication about the name on the credit card—another friend had arranged for the room—the hotel refused to let them register. So back to his car, the old car that had no passenger window and now wouldn't start. He tried to hotwire it but somehow pulled out the ignition wire instead, after a while he got the car going but it had started to rain, hard, and they had to drive back home with her getting soaked and him holding one hand out the window to help the wiper blade sweep back and forth. At home the party was still going but by now the two of them wanted to be alone, and a nasty argument broke out between the groom and a few revelers who didn't want to leave, but finally they did and the newlyweds went to sleep after the bride threw up in a hand-painted ceramic pasta bowl someone had given them. In the morning they made love and things seemed better but when she got out of bed to pee she stepped on a piece of glass from a broken bottle, maybe the one she'd broken over his head the other night or maybe one of the several that had been broken the night before, and it was back to calling the ambulance and now no one has seen them for three days but they're probably fine, just holed up together in marital bliss, not killing each other with one of the guns he keeps, sometimes things start out badly but get better, by now they're surely better, they couldn't possibly screw things up any further but maybe they could.

# *testimony*

My name is Trish and I'm not an alcoholic I'm not even twenty-one yet so I drink sometimes so what who doesn't, it's not like I've been drinking alone and I don't see any of those people here. Okay sometimes I do drink alone why not, who the fuck are you to judge you're not getting me to hold hands with a bunch of losers pumped up on coffee and cigarettes in this crummy New Jersey church basement and recite the Lord's prayer.

That reminds me. I smoked a bunch of my friend Todd's Benson and Hedges 100s last night, no wonder my throat is sore now I feel like shit with this hangover and all those stupid dreams I had about seeing my mother who's dead in a diner eating ice cream, only she turned into this disgusting half-naked drag queen with a belly button that poked out like a finger or baby penis and she had all this ghoul makeup on and then I kept driving up and down this hill with some asshole who said he was in love with me, it was like we were in that video game where you steer the car while everything whizzes by and you try to avoid the trucks and shit that appear out of nowhere and when you run into something like a tree the car flips over it's a red convertible and you and your friend sit on the grass dazed for a second then you get back in and go on.

It was like that only we didn't hit anything even though we went faster and faster and I told him to stop giving me this macho showoff shit it wasn't going to make me fall in love with him, take me home I'm not going to fuck you which is just as well because if I did I'd hate you in the morning and this way we can still be friends and I can call you up and say Let's go to that Cuban restaurant in the East Village and eat *ropa vieja* or to the Cambodian one where the waitress is in love with Tab Hunter who she saw on a TV movie and thinks is a young contemporary movie star, she just got here from the farm in Thailand. Welcome to America I said, I didn't say anything about Tab Hunter, let her get the bad news from somebody else. I could call you up to go dancing and you could swing me around and we wouldn't look stupid like those geeks last night at the club where we talked about art and serial killers and about that shithead who wrote me a poison letter because I'd made some comment that was supposed to be supportive but he took it the wrong way the paranoid asshole now there's a real alcoholic for you that guy was pathetic.

It's so hard to remember conversations when everything falls into the black hole of more drinks and twenty trips to the bathroom where the graffiti says "Every poem is a bank account accumulating interest in an existential mutual fund" and "Why am I reduced to this" and the weird woman who does handwriting analysis is in there by the mirror with her stack of raggedy papers and doesn't remember that she once accused my date of touching her ass as we walked by and then tried to get him thrown out what a laugh, who would want to touch her ass maybe the guy on 42nd St. screaming about Jesus with his Pignose amp and dirty suit but nobody else. Random words come dribbling out of the black hole the next day, Clinton Cher O.J. brothers fathers Zen AIDS clothes magazines Gauguin Long Island old boyfriends revolution Moon Zappa Bosnia M & Ms movies parties abortions salud, salud.

Sometimes when I drink I act like a slut. Like the other night I was at this fancy Harper and Row party for somebody's wine guide that just came out not that I knew him or anything, my friend Sam took me but once we'd stuffed our faces with hors-d'ouevres—meat sliced to transparency wrapped around breadsticks and some salmon shit in flowcrets on crackers—and drunk a few glasses of wine that a Central American refugee in a tuxedo kept filled, I noticed a guy staring at my blue nail polish and dumped Sam for him. I already explained about not fucking anybody because of the hatred factor but I still feel like a slut making out with guys in elevators and then going home and passing out and waking up in the middle of the night to take Advil and drink water and swear I won't do that again and wonder where my true love is and why my mother had to die on the New Jersey Turnpike two days before my eighteenth birthday which I had to spend at the fucking funeral home and talking to relatives I hate who tried to make me eat crap like potato salad and pot roast.

Last night Todd and I were in this restaurant eating pepper steak and black beans and drinking Dos Equis still relatively sober when a fucked-up old woman came in, she smelled like the bathrooms in Penn Station and looked like all the junkies and losers who hang out there with their scabby hands extended and she had the nerve to ask for a fucking dollar, like why doesn't she pick on Yuppies or somebody with money. We gave her a quarter to get rid of her and then the Puerto Rican woman came by with her crummy roses she probably sells to support her seventeen children and grandchildren so Todd bought a rose and handed it to me and our fingers touched and I pulled them away and today I looked and couldn't find it, it's probably wilted already anyway. Maybe it's in the car wherever I parked it with the congealing remains of the steak that I took the rest of to go, or maybe it's in the street somewhere or being swept up from the floor of the club by the black bald one-armed janitor, anyway the Puerto Rican woman looked creepy like the flower seller in that movie *Streetcar Named Desire* who walks through saying *Flores para los muertos*, flowers for the dead which is what I'll be before joining AA I just came here to cruise anyway but you people are a drag maybe it's in the bathroom of the club on the back of the toilet I have a distinct image of that in my mind.

# *have you seen me?*

Anne tries not to look at them when she speaks, tries to slide her eyes quickly past their faces, their bodies slumped over desks as they draw in the margins of their notebooks or cap and uncap their pens. Some of them occasionally glance up at her, but she has the overwhelming sensation that she barely exists for them; she might be a radio playing down the hall, or a plane passing overhead, or one of the invisible chorus of crickets filling the night air outside the community college. Anne talks, and keeps her eyes moving, over the students' heads, across a nauseating green and yellow jungle mural on the wall behind them with the words "Life-Long Learning" printed in a white cloud above badly misproportioned lions and apes and zebras, that look as though they were drawn by small children rather than the adult art class that used the room last semester. It saddens Anne to imagine grown men and women with flecks of paint in their hair, stepping back from the wall to gaze proudly at their terrible work.

Especially she tries not to look at the boy in the right-hand corner of the room, his long legs stuck out in front of him, his thin blond hair tucked behind his ears. If she looks at him, this is what she thinks will happen. She will say, aloud, "You have the most beautiful face I have ever seen,"and she will begin to fall into that face, to move toward it the way the dying are said to move toward the white light where everyone they have ever loved waits, beckoning and calling encouragement, and she will forget her lecture and stand dumbly before him, while the other students slowly raise their eyes and begin to snicker, and he smiles at her with his perfect large white teeth.

The boy has a styrofoam cup on top of his open note-book and sips something from it. When the cup is empty he takes a pen and begins drawing on the cup. Anne looks at the cup, at the boy's boots—black Doc Martens, heavy, solid. She imagines lying on the kitchen floor of her studio apartment, the boy standing over her, one boot placed gently on her stomach, then moving down until the toe rests between her open legs. She gazes out the row of windows, where the reflected fluorescent lights of the classroom shine grimly back at her. There is another class-room floating out there. She wants to walk through the far door and step into the air and drift down into the cool sprinkler-wet grass in the dark. She wants the boy to follow her, to kneel down and unbutton his black pants and stretch his long pale body on top of hers.

"Okay," Anne says. "That's it for tonight. Chapter Six for next week, and don't forget your comparison and contrast essays are due at the end of the month. Any questions?"

There are rarely questions, except for these: Will we be graded on this? Could you repeat the assignment?

Anne never calls on the students directly, and they never volunteer. She is afraid to call on them, afraid they will refuse to answer, and then she will be at a loss. This is only her second year of teaching. For many years before this, she was a sort of receptionist. She worked for a ball bearings manufacturer and had to keep up a "front desk appearance," wearing neat skirt and blouse ensembles and heels, though no one ever came into the tiny office where she worked except the men from the warehouse directly behind it, or the company president, whose door remained closed most of the day. She filed invoices, typed up the president's correspondence, and transferred incoming calls to him or the warehouse. She worked part-time, and the rest of the time she was a housewife. Then her husband disappeared—the way teenaged girls and little children did, without a trace, except that he took most of his belongings with him. When he didn't reappear, Anne returned to school to finish the master's degree in English she had started fifteen years before. Now she had a degree, a teaching job, and her own apartment where every night she drank too many glasses of gin and Schweppes over ice, falling asleep to the TV and waking in the middle of the night to listen to the sounds a building makes settling into the earth, preparing to outlast everyone in it. Those are Anne's thoughts at four a.m.—the permanence of walls, floorboards, toilets. At that hour she is a shadow moving across the room, slipping through the bathroom door, sitting down to pee. The pee is a small sound, a little rain on a pond; the flush of the toilet is a roaring thunderstorm .

The class ends and dissolves into disorder, desks pushed aside as the students hurry from the room. They scatter like the roaches in Anne's kitchen late at night when she flips on the light to find some Excedrin P.M. for a headache. In seconds she is alone in the room, gathering up her notes, the extra handouts she copied for students who are not there, who may not be there for weeks and will suddenly appear before her, claiming injury, illness, a mother with uterine cancer, a sister struck by a drunk driver. They will look directly into her eyes, as they have never done before, with an expression of innocent menace. I need to pass this class, they will say. I need a good grade. They will stand there until she nods, Yes, of course, I see, and then they will leave her alone.

Anne looks at the gray metal wastebasket by the door, filled with crumpled paper and soda cans and candy wrappers. Perched on top is the styrofoam cup the boy held in his hand, touched his lips to. She goes over and picks it up. She turns it around to see what he drew on the cup. It is a picture of a truck, with huge knobby wheels and a small cab perched high up with a little smiling face inside. Underneath are the words, "Monster Truck Love."

Her hand trembles. She carries the cup back to her desk, unzips the canvas shoulder bag where she keeps her books and papers, and places the cup inside. She goes to the door of the classroom, turns off the light, and stands there in the dark. Maybe the boy is waiting, she thinks. Waiting in the hall or by the pay phone near the doors leading outside or out in the cool grass. She looks toward the row of windows and sees a few trees, black against the sky. She can't see the classroom at all, or herself, standing by the door.

The door opens and she steps away in surprise. The boy is there, his thin frame outlined in the light from the hall. He turns on the light in the room, and she backs toward her desk, blinking rapidly. He gestures toward his seat.

"Forgot my pen," he mumbles.

There is a black and gold pen lying on the floor. An expensive pen, the kind given as a present to someone who would value writing with it. A present from his father? Here, son, she imagines him saying heartily. Glad you're getting an education, the father says, clapping him on the shoulder. The father is in his early forties—

a little older than Anne. He looks right through her, the way other men her age do, the way the checkout boy at the grocery store does.

"What a lovely pen," she says.

"Yeah, I guess," the boy says. He holds it in his hand, looking at it.

"You're James."

"Yeah," he says.

"Do you like the class, James?" She tries to think of something to say, to hold him there. She feels a sense of panic, as though, even though the semester has barely started, he will be gone forever if she lets him walk out the door.

"Yeah, I guess," James says. "Sure," he says. "It's kind of interesting."

He is wearing a red flannel shirt, unbuttoned, over a gray T-shirt with a bleach stain on the chest. He slips the pen into a breast pocket of the flannel shirt and turns to go.

"Wait," Anne says.

He has one hand on the doorknob; he looks back at her, over his shoulder. "Yeah?" he says.

"Ah, do you need a, a ride?"

"A ride," he repeats.

"I've passed you in my car," she says. She has crept down the street, watching him striding quickly along, head down, hands in his pockets, and books tucked under his arm. She has tried to follow him, but always another car has come up behind her and she has had to speed up and pass him, watching in her rear-view for a glimpse of his face.

"I mean," she says, and then doesn't know what she means.

"Okay," he says. He opens the door, holds it open. "After you, Ma'am," he says.

They are both silent as she drives through the dark tree-lined streets. The college is in a residential area, much greener and prettier than where Anne lives. She is struggling to pay back school loans, and she can't afford a better place. In her mind, she tells James about her money difficulties, her husband's disappearance, her loneliness. Then she mentally switches to a better conversation, a fascinating description of her life as an older, independent woman in a romantically seedy part of town. James is intrigued and asks if he might come over sometime for a drink, and she says, Well, James, I don't see why not.

James sits impassively, gazing straight ahead, occasionally looking out the side window. She can smell his sweat, sweet and acrid at the same time. His face looks very white. He has a square jawline, the faintest rash of blond beard stubble. His large hands grip the books in his lap. She tries to imagine how he lives, what he does when he is not sitting in the corner of her classroom, but she can't. He is pure and without context, radiating light into the interior of her car.

"Turn here," he says. "Pull into that driveway where the van is."

She stops behind a red Dodge van, holds on to the steering wheel while he gets out. There's no way to stop him.

"Thanks for the ride," he says.

She watches him walk toward the house. Two girls about his age sit on the steps to the porch, smoking cigarettes. One is barefoot, wearing a short black slip, and clearly pregnant. The other has on torn jeans and a blue kimono. They are both thin—even the pregnant girl has slim arms, and long pale legs—much thinner than Anne will ever be again. They move to either side of the steps to let James pass between them. They peer at the car, at Anne as she hurriedly backs out. The girl in the kimono flicks her cigarette into the grass, turns, and follows James inside.

She drives down her own street, past the corner bar with its flickering green martini glass above the door, past the closed printers and the tiny Chinese restaurant where a row of glazed ducks hangs upside-down in the dark window. They seem to be the same ducks, day after day; though she eats there often, she has never seen the cook cut one down to serve it. She parks her car and checks her metal mailbox in the lobby of the building before going up. The mail, too, is the same, day after day. Credit card offers, flyers from drugstores and supermarkets, offers for discount carpet cleaning with the faces of missing children on the reverse side. "Have You Seen Me?" the caption under their photos reads. She imagines the face of her husband in one of these photos, imagines a woman in another city leafing through her mail, suddenly confronted with the face of the man she is living with, maybe even married to.

Her apartment is on the seventh floor. There is a view of the taller apartment building opposite hers and of a billboard on top of the flat gravel-and-tar roof of the building next to that, which is a record store. The billboard advertises rock bands she has never heard of, bands she's sure her students would know. The current ad shows a half-naked woman with long purplish-black hair and gleaming skin, wearing some sort of animal pelt that barely covers her torso. Her thighs are large and muscular. Because of the ad, Anne has lately been noticing her own legs, how soft they seem, how amorphous compared to the clearly defined contours of painted flesh.

She stands naked before the full-length mirror nailed to the back of the bathroom door and sees a lump of flesh being gradually pulled downward by gravity, crowned by a small perplexed face with dark blue eyes. This is what James would see, if he were to take off her clothes. This is what her husband saw for years, what he walked away from without a note or a word of explanation. She had returned from work late, after stopping at the grocery store for ground beef to make tacos. She had opened their apartment door and called his name into the silence. He wasn't on the couch where he usually was, watching TV with his hand in a bowl of reduced-salt potato chips. His hunting rifle was gone, his college wrestling trophies, and his motivational cassette tapes with titles like Effective Public Speaking and Low-Stress Success. Where his "Employee of the Year" award from the furniture store had hung there was only a shiny nail, bent down as though he'd struggled and finally yanked the plaque off the wall. There was no sign of him, except for the open bag of potato chips in the cupboard and a bottle of Miller Lite in the fridge. And his photo was still on the fridge door. He was wearing a long-sleeved camouflage shirt and blue jeans, and he was down on one knee, holding a dead turkey. After she looked in the closet and saw he had taken his clothes, saw the tangle of empty hangers next to her dresses and blouses, Anne had torn the photo into little pieces. She dropped them into the trash compactor, along with the chips and the bottle of beer, which made a satisfying noise as it was smashed down. Then she made six tacos—spicy, the way he hated them—and ate every one.

She pulls on a blue terrycloth robe, belts it, and goes to make herself a ham and cheese sandwich. She pours a drink and stands at the counter that separates the kitchen from the rest of the room, drinking and taking bites of the sandwich. Then she turns off all the lights, takes her glass and the bottles of gin and Schweppes to the couch and sits there in the dark, looking at the pulled curtains of windows across the street, lit from within by lamps and TV's. After four drinks she takes off the couch pillows and pulls out the sofabed and lies down, not bothering to get the top sheet and blanket from the closet, and curls up listening for the sound of roaches creeping across the the counter to carry away the crumbs of her sandwich.

The next week, after class, James is standing outside the glass doors of the building when she emerges.

"Hey," he says. "Could I get a ride again?"

"All right," Anne says, trying to sound casually friendly; indifference is more than she can manage.

She has spent all week thinking about him, waiting to see him again. She is wearing a new outfit she bought at Ross—Dress for Less, the TV commercial had said, showing attractive, confident women striking poses in vibrant dresses and pantsuits. Anne has on a long, colorful skirt, with a blue silk blouse that matches the blue in the skirt. She feels conspicuous in these clothes, since she usually wears pantsuits in navy or beige or brown, neutral colors and patterns that don't stand out. But no one seems to have noticed the change—not the other teachers in the faculty lounge, who mostly ignore her anyway, engrossed as they usually are in chatting amiably or viciously about the stupidity of their students while consuming chips and diet sodas; and not the students, who tonight were concerned with exactly how few pages they could turn in for next week's essay. James doesn't seem to notice, either. He gets into her car and sits as silently as before, until the turn for his street comes.

"Here it is," he says.

This time there are no girls smoking on the steps. There are lights on in the house, though, and there is loud music thumping inside—repetitive, throbbing, hypnotic. James thanks her again and slams the car door, and then he is swallowed by the house, by whatever mysterious primitive rituals are taking place in there.

The next week he is waiting again. Anne knows where to turn by now, and so the entire ride is spent in silence. She pulls into the driveway—it's empty, the van is gone, the house dark and silent—and waits for him to get out, for the intensity she feels in his presence to ebb away until she is dead and numb once more. The thought of driving home, of walking into her empty apartment, fills her with despair.

James doesn't get out of the car; he sits there, humming under his breath.

"James," she says. "We're here."

"Uh, do you want to come in?" he says.

Her heart begins pounding in her ears. She is afraid she only imagined him speaking; she looks at him and he is humming again, looking out the car window toward the house. His big thumbs tap out a nervous beat on the books in his lap and then stop abruptly; he turns and looks at her, smiles, looks away.

"What?" she says.

"You know," he says. "Like for a drink. There's tea, or milk, or some vodka in the freezer."

"Yes, thank you," she says. "I believe I would like something to drink."

She follows him from the car, feeling as though she is floating across the grass. The yard is uncut, weedy. The new skirt, which she is wearing again, makes a pleasant swishing sound. She imagines the weeks to come—the classroom where he will undress her with his eyes without the other students knowing, the long nights of love afterwards, when they will tear at each other's bodies like two animals, wild with desire.

On the top step leading to the house she trips and falls against a beat-up wicker chair with a musty-smelling cushion. Her hands sink into the dampness of the cushion, and she feels a small shooting pain in her left wrist. James, she notices as she rights herself, has made no move to help her catch her balance. He simply watches her, and she feels suddenly foolish. He probably only wants to ask her something about the essay he turned in tonight, a scant two pages instead of the required three to five. Maybe he wants an extension to finish it, and will give her some story about working three jobs or a funeral several states away. Maybe he is the father of the baby the pregnant girl is carrying, and needs to arrange an independent study for the rest of the semester in order to help care for it. Anything is possible, Anne thinks. Anything except the idea that he might be attracted to her. But it's too late. James has finally moved closer, a concerned expression on his face, and touched her awkwardly, grazingly, on one elbow, sending a current of heat shooting along her arm.

"Whoa," he says. "You okay?"

"Of course," she says. He turns to the door, fumbling with a key, and she has to resist the urge to touch his thin shoulder blades, to run the palm of her hand down his spine.

There's no rug in the living room and no furniture except for a fraying green armchair next to a stereo with CD's scattered on the floor around it. There's a fireplace with a litter box inside it, filled with cat turds. Above the mantle a mounted buffalo head stares down, wearing a necklace of chili lights. James leads her to the kitchen, where they sit on stools beside a blue-tiled counter—there's no kitchen table—and drink shots of vodka from large plastic cups. James hums. Anne tries to think of something to say, some way to help either of them. Mutely, she downs the shots James pours, and then holds out her cup for more.

Soon she is drunk. She remembers a cassette her husband used to play—something called Out on a Limb: Taking Chances With Your Life. "There is no such thing as a safe risk," she hears the narrator's smooth, persuasive voice saying in her head. "You are going to have to go out on that limb, and, folks, it may not hold you! That's the truth!" He had gone on, saying something about climbing trees and lightning and human ancestors walking upright for the first time; the memory is vague, since Anne had never really paid attention to her husband's tapes. Maybe there had been one titled To Hell With Everything, and that was why he had left her. Well, she thinks. I can't just curl up and die like some wounded animal.

She stands, goes over to James on his stool, and leans toward him. She gazes up at his face, too far away to kiss, and then sags against his skinny chest.

"Hey," he says, giving her a little push backwards.

"You're beautiful," she tells him, swaying before him.

"You have the most beautiful face I've ever seen."

She puts her hands on his thighs, leans forward, and kisses him quickly. His mouth tastes like lemons. She gazes into his beautiful eyes, which have tiny red veins running through the whites. He cuts his eyes away, toward the living room, and jiggles his leg against the stool.

"Uh—" he says.

"It's all right," she says. She has climbed up the tree, inched her way along the branch. It is not going to hold her. She falls to her knees and wraps her arms around his big boots.

"Uh—" he says, and gets off the stool, extricating himself. She sits on the floor, looking up at him.

"It's like this," he says. "My roommates said I should invite you in and see what happened. They said you probably had the hots for me. I told them it was bullshit. We bet five bucks on it."

It's the most she has ever heard him say.

"Oh," she says. She notices the floor is sticky, lifts her hands, and puts them in her lap.

"I guess it was a dumb thing to do," he says.

"Oh, God," Anne says. She imagines them, the two girls and James, standing in the living room and laughing. She sees him describing how his teacher tripped on the front steps, how she got drunk, how pathetic she looked sitting on their kitchen floor. "How could you do this?" she says.

"Hey, I'm sorry." He sounds genuinely contrite, though he refuses to look at her; he stares at the empty cups, picks one up and crumples it in his right hand, then hooks it into a wastebasket at the end of the counter.

"It's all right." Of course it isn't all right, Anne thinks. It isn't, but she's not going to tell him that.

"This won't affect my grade, will it?" James says. "Oh, shit, I didn't mean that like it sounds. I'm such an asshole." He looks more and more miserable; he looks like he might cry any minute. "Excuse my language," he says, his voice tremulous.

She gets up, holding onto the stool for balance, and

backs away from him. She looks past him out the window. Out there, in that other kitchen, she sees the back of
his head, his shoulders. She sees herself facing him. She
is wearing another new blouse, a bright green one. Her
image in the glass seems to shimmer and vibrate, like a
heat mirage.

"Do you think I'm attractive, James?" she says.

James reaches for the vodka, pours another shot into
the remaining cup and offers it to her. "Sure, I guess," he
says. "It's just that, no offense or anything, you're kind
of old." He looks at her, his face reddened and blotchy
from drinking, an ordinary, handsome boy's face. There
is actually a tear in the corner of one eye, a glittery drop-
let about to spill over, that he wipes away with the back
of his hand.

For a moment she imagines pulling him to the floor,
lifting his shirt and licking his white belly, his nipples,
moving up to his mouth to taste his thick pink tongue.
She knows this isn't going to happen, now or ever. She is
going to thank James politely for sharing his vodka and
walk calmly away from him, down the stairs of his house
without tripping. She is going to get into her car and drive
home, carefully, then open the sofabed and turn on the
TV. And tomorrow night she is going to put on one of her
new soft blouses and the colorful skirt, and walk to the
bar down the street from her apartment, where no one
under twenty-one is allowed. There are always single men
in a bar. They go there out of thirst, like beasts to a water-
ing hole. They sit alone, hunched over their drinks, not
wanting to go home. They are filled with loneliness, and
grateful when a woman speaks to them, so grateful they
will offer to buy her a drink, will look into her eyes and
tell her she is beautiful. They will ask, timidly, whether
they might walk her home, whether they might come in.
They will tremble, aching to touch her.

"Old," she repeats. "I'm thirty-eight."

"Yeah," he says.

She sees that James is trembling now, his shoulders

shaking, sobs gathering at the back of his throat. In a minute he'll break down, Anne thinks; he'll find himself crying like a little kid in front of his teacher. She takes her purse from the counter, turns away toward the door.

"Oh, poor baby," she says. "You don't know anything, do you?"

# angels

Loren has decided to let me keep the apartment and to find another place for himself. I told him that Sasha won't even answer my phone calls anymore, so there is no need for him to be jealous and leave. It's over with Sasha, I said, but Loren says Sasha had nothing to do with it.

I would have left anyway, he says. I'm not right for you.

You mean you don't love me anymore, I say.

We are sitting on the deck in uncomfortable wrought-iron chairs the landlord gave us, along with a glass-topped round table. I watch Loren jiggle his leg under the table, something he does when he is lying.

Of course I love you, he says.

No you don't.

You have so many problems, he says. He doesn't look at me when he says it.

You have problems too. No one will buy your paintings. You don't make enough money. You have psoriasis, and bursitis in your shoulder from playing softball. You're allergic to strawberries.

You know what I mean. You have all these—compulsions. I never know what you're going to do, what's going to freak you out or suddenly attract you and send you veering off in a different direction. I want somebody normal, Loren says. Somebody I can have normal sex with. Somebody I can—satisfy.

Sex with Loren is worse than normal, I think, watching him gaze out at the houses around us. Everyone's windows look black, you can't see in. Sasha's window, down the hill, has the curtains closed. Sex with Loren is boring, like doing the dishes. Almost every night, at almost the same time, we fuck the same way. I suck him while he lies back, and when he gets hard I lie on my back and he fucks me, and then he licks me to try and get me to come.

Just out of curiosity, Loren says. How was it with Sasha? Did you come with him?

No.

What the fuck was the point, then?

Why are you yelling? I thought you weren't jealous.

I'm not jealous, Loren says, still yelling. I'm just sick and tired of dealing with you and your trips. I'm sick of you being afraid of everything. I'm sick of worrying about you, wondering whether you'll get home in one piece, whether something will happen to you.

He stops yelling, stands up, and leans against the wood railing of the deck, looking down at me. I'm sorry your stepfather molested you, he says. And I'm sorry you were raped last year. I know those were terrible things. But I don't know what to do about any of it. I just want a girlfriend, he says. I want to have some fun once in a while. You're just no goddamned fun, Fran.

That's the thing he says that hurts me the most.

I don't mind being alone. There is no one to annoy, no one to scowl at me if I leave my jeans and underwear on the bathroom floor. I can sleep all day, and Loren won't be there when I wake up in the afternoon, telling me I should do something constructive. I sleep until two or three, get up and shower and eat, listen to music until it's time to go to work.

The part I like best about work is the first few seconds of each phone call, when the person on the other end thinks it might be personal. Hello? They say. Then there is a brief, expectant pause, before I have to say Good evening, Mrs. _____, or Mr. _____ , or sometimes Ms. As soon as I say that, they know it isn't really them I want to talk to. Often they hang up before I can go on and ask for a few minutes of their time. Just a survey, I say, if they give me the chance. Do you belong to a political party? Do you own a microwave oven? Often, when I am walking to or from work, I will look at people's faces and wonder if we have spoken to each other without knowing it, if I have said their names and they have answered No thank you or I don't have time or All right, how long will this take? Maybe they have told me things, maybe I know things about them.

Tonight I spoke with a woman who answered the phone crying. It's over, John, she said. For God's sake don't call me again.

I hung up without saying anything. I thought about her all the way home, and I am still thinking about her. I made up a story to explain what she said. I decided she was married to John, that he will not stop calling her to try and get her back. She still loves him, but she is afraid that if he comes back, things will be as bad as they were before. I imagine picking up the phone and saying to

Loren, For God's sake don't call me again. But he hasn't called. He's been gone a month.

I think about dialing Sasha's number. But I can hear him saying Fran, for God's sake don't call me again. Sasha would not be crying. He would be cold and reasonable, he would explain that he is seeing someone else. I saw her once, a tall woman with short straight blonde hair. I looked into Sasha's living room window with my binoculars one night, and she was standing beside his piano. She rested one hand on his shoulder, and with the other she turned the pages of music while he played. She stood where I had once knelt down, naked, handcuffed to the piano leg. I watched her stop turning the pages and climb onto Sasha's lap, straddling him, pressing her breasts against his chest while they kissed. Sasha stood up, and she wrapped her legs around his waist. Then he walked to the window, still carrying her, and closed the curtains.

I go out to the deck, but his curtains are closed again. I can see a light through them, so he is probably home. He is probably fucking the blonde woman, making her come. I go back inside and lie down on the bathroom floor and finger myself, and imagine that Sasha's dick is throbbing inside me, that he is saying Please, Frannie, come for me, let your sweet cunt come, let it go, give it to me. Little cunt, little whore. My stepfather comes into the bathroom, which I forgot to lock, and catches me masturbating. I sit up, grab for my underwear but he gets it first. He's blocking the door; I hear it click behind him. He pushes me back down on the floor. I don't come when he fucks me. I only come now, years later, thinking about it. And then I hate myself even more than I hate him.

Nicky comes over to help me dye my hair. She puts on plastic gloves, mixes the dye and developer, and massages it in. It smells terrible. We had to strip my hair first, since I am going from dark brown to blonde. The woman

at the beauty store thought it was a bad idea. It ruins
your hair, she said. Dries it out. Do you want it to break
off? she said. I would have put the dye back, but Nicky
set it down hard on the counter and took out a credit
card. Conditioner, Nicky said. And some good shampoo.
You know, that protein-keratin stuff. Nicky is good at
shopping, at talking to clerks.

Marilyn Monroe, Nicky says, when we're done.

Not quite, I say. I'm too skinny.

I hate you, Nicky says. If only I could stop eating, she
says, and looks at herself in the mirror. No wonder he
won't touch me. I really am a fat pig.

Your husband is the pig, I say. I look at us together. I
don't recognize myself. My eyes look darker. I look into
Nicky's eyes in the mirror.

Nicky, I say. Do you have orgasms?

He won't make love to me anymore, Nicky says. He
used to make me so happy. She starts to cry.

I'm sorry, Nicky.

I really am going to kill him, she says.


The bartender brings us another round of dry martinis. I've never had a martini, though I know how to make
one; my stepfather showed me. I would fix drinks for
him and my mother and their friends, and bring them
on a tray, and he would pat my ass and say, Isn't she
something? Everyone would look at me, at my face burning with shame, and think I was blushing.

Nicky usually can't get away at night, but the Army
sent her husband on a business trip to Fort Ord, and she
got a friend to come over and watch her kids. I try to
imagine being Nicky, stuck on an Army base with a violent husband, not knowing how to get out. I try to be
happy that I'm living alone, but I'm not happy. I'm starting to get afraid again, the way I was after the rape. On
the street, men stare at me, at my white-blonde hair. They
say things. Hey, cunt. Hey, is your pussy blonde too?

Last week a man followed me for half a block, and I ran the rest of the way home. When I got to my door, I couldn't catch my breath. I collapsed on the front steps, in front of the iron gate, and thought my heart would explode. I thought maybe the man was still following me, that I would feel his hands pulling down my jeans, moving the crotch of my panties aside so he could shove it in me without taking them off. The next day I couldn't go to work. I couldn't even get dressed.

Hey, Nicky says. Isn't this great? Isn't this band great?

The band is playing zydeco music. A man is singing in French, and couples are dancing in the room next to the bar. Nicky dances in her seat, her eyes glued to the couples. I know she wants somebody to ask her to dance, but nobody does.

We have more martinis. The band takes a break, then comes back. The bar gets crowded, begins to smell of alcohol and sweat and perfume. The music seems to get louder. It fills up the inside of my head, not leaving any space to think.

Fuck it, Nicky says, getting up. I'm going to dance by myself.

I follow her into the next room and find a wall to lean against. Nicky starts doing really old dances, like my mother used to do. In the car sometimes, when a song she liked came on the radio, my mother would start jerking back and forth, waving her arms. My mother loves dancing and parties and drinking. She always drank too much to notice what was going on. Or maybe that's why she drank. We never talked about it.

Nicky looks like she's having fun. I think about what Loren said. I wonder if Loren is somewhere right now, dancing with a normal girl, someone who knows how to have fun. I lean harder against the the wall, wanting it to turn into a door, a door that will lead into a dark room where no one can see me, where I can lie down and be still as a stone.

You wanna dance?

He has on a black pullover sweatshirt with a hood in back; two strings dangle down in front. He has lank black hair that falls over one eye, and pale skin. He looks my age, or younger, more like a boy than a man.

I'm Matt, he says.

As soon as we start dancing, the song ends. We stand there a little uncertainly, and when the next song is a slow one he turns away. But he is only pulling off his sweatshirt. The skin of his back glows for a moment when his T-shirt rides up. He throws his sweatshirt onto one of the stools along the wall and moves towards me. I lean against his thin chest as we sway back and forth. He isn't wearing cologne; he just smells like skin and sweat and soap.

I don't exactly remember getting home. There was a conversation with Nicky, a cab ride. Dropped keys, a lamp knocked over, a cube of ice sliding across the kitchen counter. Matt's body is smooth all over. He lies sleeping on my bed, his mouth a little open, his dark hair in his face. He looks beautiful and white and clean, like someone made out of soap. I don't think we fucked. I remember taking my clothes off while he watched me, then lying on the bed while he removed his boots, his thick white socks, his sweatshirt and fatigues. He wasn't wearing any underwear. He lay down next to me, and I took off his T-shirt. Then I think we fell asleep.

I put my hand between my legs and start to rub myself. The lamp is on, and the blinds are pulled up on the sliding glass doors that lead to the deck. Against the blackness of the glass, I can faintly see myself and Matt and the bed, looking as though it is floating outside on the air. I'm still not used to my hair; I wave my arm to see if the blonde ghost on the glass waves her arm, too. I press down hard on my clit with my middle finger, getting more excited, and then close my eyes.

115

I'm floating for a long time. Then I feel a hand on my breast, a thumb and forefinger lightly twisting my nipple. I feel breathing on my face.

Hi, he says. He puts his palm on my stomach. I open my eyes and look at him.

Don't stop, he says.

He could be anyone—a junkie, a serial killer. Maybe he will tie me up and rape me and then strangle me, and I will lie here for days, or longer. Loren and Sasha will come to my funeral. Sasha will bring his new girlfriend, and afterwards they will go home and fuck on the floor, clawing at each other. My mother and stepfather will be there, and they will both be drunk. Nicky will write a poem about me and read it, crying, and no one will listen to her. She will go home to her husband and cry some more, and he will slap her and call her a fat cow. I think about how good it would feel to be dead, not to know any of that. I think about John and the woman crying over the phone.

I look again at our reflections. We're angels, I think. I'm already dead. I watch one angel propped on an elbow, rubbing the stomach of the other one. I watch the black air around them, the empty space on all sides that's always there no matter what they do. He touches her thighs, puts a finger inside her, moves it slowly until she starts quivering and her legs begin to stiffen. I watch the arches of her feet. I watch him roll over on top of her, his white ass curving, a moon above the sleeping houses. But I can't watch her come. Because at the second it happens I feel him pushing inside of me, filling me. I hear him singing in my ear, and I fall a long way, all the way down until I land on the bed, feel it solid beneath me, and cry out.

# flash suppressor

He would always try to find a hiding place in the camp at night, so he was curled up behind some boxes of C-rations when the sentry fell asleep and the VC crawled in under the wires and started killing guys in their beds; he heard something in his dream and there was a VC with an AK-47 trying to open one of the boxes. He jumped up and grabbed the weapon by the flash suppressor— the metal tube that hid the flash of bullets fired at night— and it and the barrel came off in his hand so he beat the VC to death with it. The metal burned his palm and took most of the skin off. Later he did three more tours and later still sat on a piece of styrofoam at the corner of Jones and Eddy in San Francisco, drinking Canadian Club, taking a bead on the locals at night with an imaginary starlight scope—whores and drunks and gooks everywhere and drug dealers selling to punks and faggots dressed like women. Once he had let one named Lucille suck him in the bathroom of some bar, not realizing at first, and Lucille looked up and said baby what happened to your hand, then he saw the texture of Lucille's skin under the heavy pancake, oh he said, spilled a pan of boiling water once and Lucille said honey that must of hurt and he said I never felt a fucking thing then or now and it was true he couldn't come so finally Lucille went out and he lay down and curled himself into the space between the toilet and the wall.

# *gaps*

I wake up at five a.m., not the worst time to wake up but not an encouraging sign for the coming day. Five a.m. means a bad hangover. Three or four a.m. means the day is going to be canceled, because I will spend it throwing up until there is nothing left, crouched in front of the toilet while the cat stands with her paws on the edge and peers with me into the bowl. Some drinkers, I am told, sleep like a baby from the time they pass out until the afternoon of the next day and wake up feeling perfectly fine. The guy next to me, whoever he is, must be one of those.

I get up and head for the tin of Extra Strength Tylenol in my purse on the kitchen table. I have to hunt for my purse because a trash can has been emptied on the table. Hardened cat turds, grains of litter, dust balls, a soaked coffee filter, crushed Coors cans. I remember the guy in my bed saying Coors was swill. Or maybe he said swell. After I take the Tylenol, I crawl back into bed and try to mentally distract myself from the realization that I have once again taken a wrong turn, bumped off the highway and landed upside-down in a ditch beside a dead-end road. The Bates Motel is at the end of the road, and Norman is sharpening his knife.

I try to remember fucking this guy. I know I did because I stepped on a dried condom getting out of bed.

There are these gaps.

"Am I trying to get you into bed? No. Would I? In a minute. In a minute. So would any of the guys at this party. I ain't trying to screw you. I just wanna talk to you."

"Relax, Freddy," I say. "We're on the same wavelength here."

Freddy's sunglasses fall from his bald forehead and land on his nose. He puts his cigar back in his mouth. Freddy is drunk. He's also old. We sit down together at the kitchen table and eat some ice cream with chocolate sauce. Freddy keeps pouring more sauce into my bowl.

"My thesis was on rape," a woman leaning against the refrigerator says, to nobody.

A man in a tuxedo T-shirt is videotaping the party. Earlier, Freddy took a picture of me with a guy I'd just met. We put our arms around each other and smiled. Old friends.

This is one party I'll remember.

Freddy gets up from the table, and my old friend takes his place. I ask him his name. I don't give a shit what his name is. What I really want to know is whether he has any more of the joint he passed me earlier, and if he's seen any hard liquor yet.

"Harley," he says.

"Is that a first name or a last name?"

"It's just a name. Like Cher."

Cher has had electrolysis all over her body. If I dyed my hair black and got a perm and a nose job and maybe a year-long stretch on the rack, I'd look just like her.

"Say, Harley. Is there anything besides beer to drink at this party?"

"You got a jacket?" he says. "I'll take you around the corner to the Phoenix. Great jukebox. Frank Sinatra. Ma Rainey. Siouxie and the Banshees."

The guy with the VCR cam is in the hall. He films our exit. Six hours later I wake up on a rug that used to be a polar bear.

Maybe I shot it. Anything is possible.


Look at it this way. My brain, at thirty, is becoming a *tabula rasa*. No longer corrupted by false knowledge or perverted by a sick culture, I can return to innocence. Clean and blank as a baby. Or maybe a cadaver. When you die, your fingernails go on for a while. And your hair. Your roots grow out and you look like shit. Probably no one wants to date you.

Once, I'm told, I got onstage in a karaoke bar, drunk, and sang my heart out. I sang "Gypsies, Tramps, and Thieves" and brought the house down. Once I was driving around with some guy and we picked up a pregnant woman who had her baby in his back seat, at least that was his explanation for the blood I found there the next morning. Maybe we'd picked up a woman and nailed her with a ballpene hammer, and I'd be put away for life. Eventually I'd come up for parole and the parole board would ask if I felt any remorse, and I'd have to tell them, not really. Once I did end up in jail for drunk and disorderly.

Mostly I end up in bed, though.

I could almost write a book. Chapter One: Evening. A woman who bears a striking resemblance to Cher stands holding a drink. She sips it leisurely. Interesting people talk to her. Through her conversational skills she conveys that she is an intelligent, rational human being. She has a few more drinks. Chapters two to thirteen are blank. In chapter fourteen she sits up and looks for her clothes.

My therapist says we have to stop our sessions at the end of this month, because she's got a new job doing court-referred cases. Molested women, battered women; no drunks or sluts. Once I did wake up with bruises, but they faded. She suggested AA, but I don't want to quit drinking; I just want to remember things, I want a few answers.

These are the questions I have: Who am I when I'm drunk? Did I come when we fucked? Did you? I want to know what it felt like. Why did I like you last night when I can't stand you now?

I watched a woman at a party once. She stood leaning against a table of food, painfully shy, obviously miserable. Somebody told me she was a recovered alcoholic. In the old days, when she drank, she was the life of the party. I pitied her, standing there eating tortilla chips, overweight, and gaining more by the minute. I watched her until someone passed me a bottle of tequila and a lime wedge. The next thing I knew I was in a bathroom, throwing up. A man wiped my face with a cold washcloth, then turned me around and opened his fly. I started hitting him and he left, and then I sat on the bathroom floor and cried until a girl I knew came in with some coke.

When I was nineteen, a man in the lobby of a fancy hotel offered me a hundred dollars to fuck him. I was drunk so I said okay; he took me to a gas station down the street into the women's bathroom and had me suck his cock, then fucked me over the toilet. This is what I remember about him: he was a Taurus, he had green eyes, he was uncircumcised. He left me in the bathroom, saying he had to go get his wallet, and drove off. Once I had sex with my boyfriend in a laundromat bathroom, but I forget what that was like. I remember the laundromat, though; it was in Frederick, Maryland, near a farmhouse where my boyfriend and I were living with too many other people, taking too many drugs. The stereo was always blasting. Sometimes the Black Angus cows in the field across the road would amble over and line up at the fence to listen. Drinking wasn't any big deal; we had a freezer full of Ecstasy. Once we all stayed high for about a week. At the end of the week one of the people in the house went into the woods and came back with his body smeared with blackberries, waving a gun, so we switched to hitting up heroin. Then the women cooked a big vegetarian meal, and everybody spent a night coming down, throwing up and talking and nodding on the heroin.

Those were the days.

Freddy just turned seventy. He's celebrating at the Ninth Inning with me, two hookers, a certified nut, and Harley. The nut weighs about three hundred pounds and writes poems with titles like "Steady Pussy" and "Lament of the Lonely Fudge Packer." He worked for the government until one day when he flipped out and thought he was a horse. Now he travels between California and Connecticut, where his parents live. When he's in Connecticut he substitute teaches high school social studies.

Harley and I have been an item since I woke up on his bear rug. He has an apartment full of dead animals—deer heads, moose antlers, rabbits' feet. The rabbits' skins are all over the apartment on little tables, like fur doilies. I believe in animal rights so it's a sore point between us.

"You look better since you dyed your hair black," Freddy says. He has an arm around each hooker. Later he'll take them back to his crummy room which has nothing in it but a bed, a refrigerator, and a porn poster, and do coke all night. I wonder if he can fuck anymore. It's probably not good for you to fuck on coke at that age. I worry about Freddy.

"Thanks, Freddy," I say, not mentioning that it will wash out in about six weeks.

Harley orders more drinks, and I reach for my seventh Campari and soda. I'm supposed to work in the morning, but I'm already planning to be too sick to go in. I'm probably getting fired soon, anyway. Luckily there are a million temp agencies in the city, and I've only been dumped by four so far; besides I can type eighty words a minute, and I also spell. You'd be surprised how many people can't.

"Is your pussy hair black, too?" the nut asks me.

"None of your fucking business," Harley says.

"Just wondering," the nut says. He puts on an offended look. "It's not like I was asking to suck it or anything," he says.

Harley hauls off and hits him. That's another sore point between us; Harley is kind of violent. "Take an eye for an eye and the whole world will be blind," I told him once, quoting Gandhi. "In the world of the blind, the man with one eye is king," he said. I was impressed, but maybe he didn't make it up himself. The nut staggers back under the blow and starts screaming, "Don't hit me! Don't hit me!"

"Leave him alone," Freddy says, "it's my birthday party."

"Tell her you're sorry," Harley says to the nut. He's got him by the collar, half-bent over the bar. The nut apologizes to me, and Harley lets him go. He reaches for my hand and pulls me against him and kisses me.

Harley is crazy in love with me, or so he says. He's a sincere person so I guess he means it, but I don't really know what he means by "love," or "crazy," or even "me." I mean, what is love, anyway? I know that sounds like a stupid question, but I really don't know the answer. I guess I love Freddy, but I don't want to fuck him. I thought I was in love with my boyfriend when we all lived at the farmhouse, but I can barely remember now what he looked like. He said he loved me, but he ran off

124

with a gay lawyer who lived on Capitol Hill. It seems like love should be better than that. I think Harley means we have good sex and can drink together, and also he's been lonely and fucked up since his parents died in a boating accident two years ago. I think he means he likes my ass and I'll let him tie me up. I think he has blackouts like I do, and it's nice to see somebody in the morning who doesn't tell you what an asshole you were the night before since she doesn't remember the night before.

The bartender brings out a cake and a bottle of champagne. We all sing "Happy Birthday" and toast Freddy. He's drunk; he has two cigars going in ashtrays on the bar. He pulls out another one from his shirt pocket and lights it up, and the hookers kiss him on each cheek, and Freddy cries and says he loves us all.


Cher has a tattoo. You can see it in the music video where she's singing and dancing in front of a big ship with about a thousand sailors leering at her; it's on her ass. I won't tell you what it is; you can look for yourself. Harley has a lightning bolt on his chest. One night, when I've been drinking gin and eating codeine tablets left over from oral surgery, I decide I want a copy of it on my ass.

Harley knows a tattoo artist who works out of his kitchen; we call him up and he says to come on over. Standing in his kitchen while he draws a stencil of the design on me, I feel faint and pass out. A minute later I come to, slumped in a chair, Harley and the artist and his wife standing over me.

"It happens even to big strong men," the artist tells me reassuringly. I haven't told him about the gin and codeine; he's a Buddhist.

The artist's wife is a Buddhist, too. She's Japanese and barely speaks English. She has roses tattooed up and down her arms and across her breasts. Tattoos look better on women; on men there's all that hair. Fat men are even worse. Harley knows a fat hairy guy with tattoos

125

all over him. Some of the tattoos are done in black light inks. He looks like a bad psychedelic poster. Imagine fucking a guy like that; he probably has black lights all over his bedroom. His girlfriend designed the stuff on his right arm, so I guess what they say is true; there really is someone for everyone.

The artist sets a board across two chairs, and I lie down on it on my stomach and pull up my skirt. It doesn't hurt as much as I thought it would; it's not nearly as bad as electrolysis.

"Did you hear about the woman who had the Chicago fire tattooed on one knee and the devil on the other?" the artist says over the buzzing of the needle. "She looked like hell."

"Ha, ha," I say. I hope he doesn't know any light bulb jokes.

Harley holds my hand; he looks all choked up, like he's about to cry. We both feel a little like we're getting married. A tattoo lasts longer than marriage; when Harley and I break up I'll still have his tattoo.

Harley says I shouldn't think like that, but I do. One more sore point. "Look no further," Harley says, "you've found the man of your dreams." But I never remember my dreams; all I remember is stuff I'd rather forget, like the guy when I was nineteen, or like my father being drunk and coming after me with his cowboy belt. It was tan, with a big turquoise and silver buckle, and it had TEXAS worked into the leather in silver studs on one side. Luckily for me, he was too drunk and missed me most of the time, but when those studs landed it hurt like hell.

Harley, even though he's violent, has never laid a hand on me.

My therapist, before she dumped me, always used to say, "What does it feel like?" I would start talking and she would say, "But you're intellectualizing. What does it feel like, where do you feel it?"

"I don't feel it anywhere," I'd say. "I'm trying to explain it to you, if you'll just listen." I wasn't paying her to help me feel my feelings; I can do that anytime. I just wanted some answers. I wanted to know if you really change when you get older, or if you just have to resign yourself to the way you've always been. I wanted to know why I'm still single, when everybody I grew up with has been married and divorced already. I wanted to know why I drink. I've never been able to trust anyone who doesn't drink. The worst are the ones who used to drink; it's like they've been saved by Jesus, they can't shut up about it.

Freddy just went on the wagon. He says the drinking was killing him.

"C'mon, Freddy," I say. "Life is killing you."

Now, Freddy says, he can use all the money he's saving to go to the track. Freddy's on Social Security; I can't figure out how he affords hookers.

"A young gal like you," Freddy says. "You should get off the booze, get married, have a couple of kids. Harley is goofy about you. Why don't you two get married?"

We're sitting in the Ninth Inning; I'm having scotch and Freddy is having Calistoga with lime.

"People are different now than they used to be," I tell Freddy. "They don't get married just like that." Freddy has been married three times. His first wife died, and his second and third wives left him. He has pictures of them all in his wallet, along with all the hookers and girlfriends he could get to pose naked for him. A lot of them did. "Buy me another, Freddy," I say. "I'm out of money."

"Promise you'll pay me back?"

"One way or another," I shrug. I've had a few scotches, it comes out easily. Freddy will buy me drinks all night now if I want him to. Maybe I'll even fuck him, and since I won't remember it I won't feel funny seeing him later. Maybe, in fact, I've already fucked him.

A tall blonde woman in a Giants cap walks in and heads to the back of the bar, where the bathrooms are.

Freddy leers at her as she goes by.

"You're my kind of woman," he tells her. He says that all the time; it's amazing how often they fall for it. She smiles at him and keeps walking.

I'm starting to feel nauseous; I haven't eaten since lunch. I have a pack of Eagle snacks with my next scotch.

That's the last thing I remember: the blonde, and the Eagle snacks. I'm lying in bed, and I'm afraid to open my eyes to see where I am. I listen to the breathing next to me and try to figure out if it's Freddy's, or even human. If it's Freddy and we fucked, at least it didn't kill him. I'd hate to wake up with a corpse, like Jane Fonda in *The Morning After*.

I wonder if Freddy got me to pose naked for his wallet gallery. I lie there listening, my eyes glued shut, feeling worse and worse. I think about being as old as Freddy, living on a fixed income in a lonely room, picking up guys at the Ninth Inning. I think about having a wallet—a big wallet—full of pictures of all the guys I ever fucked, flashing it to younger guys to prove I'm still desirable. Cher had a younger guy, a bartender, but he dumped her. If even Cher couldn't keep a younger guy, how will I manage? I know how: I'll sit at the end of the bar, I'll wear too much makeup and a funny hat, and the bartender will lie that I look gorgeous and play bar dice with me. Nobody else will talk to me, except for old men too drunk to make any sense. When the Inning closes I'll totter home to sleep, and when it opens at six a.m. I'll be there.

My head is killing me. I want to get up and look for some aspirin, but I feel paralyzed. The person—thing—next to me groans, puts its arm across my breasts. I can feel its sour breath on my face. I'm just about to scream when it asks me my name and if I'd like a cup of coffee.

"No, thanks," I say. I get up, not looking at him, and throw on my clothes. I take a cab straight to Harley's and let myself in with the key he gave me. Then I take every dead animal I can find and stuff them all into the garbage can at the bottom of his stairs, crawl into bed beside him, and wait for him to wake up.

128

# bedtime story

Once upon a time, in a bed a little smaller than this one, a man and woman were fucking doggie style, the woman had a collar around her neck and the man was growling, biting her neck as he fucked her from behind and held the choke chain from her collar in one hand. After they both sweated and moaned and growled and whimpered and came, the man got up and led the woman on her hands and knees to the bathroom to wash up. He led her back to the living room and attached the chain to a metal ring screwed into the wall, and all day the woman stayed there naked while the man read the Sunday *New York Times* and made phone calls and watched "Wide World of Sports" and snacked, sometimes reaching down from the couch to stroke the woman's hair or feed her a little cheese or salted peanuts. The woman grew so excited by all this that she crawled over to the man's leg and started rubbing herself against him, but each time she did the man hit her with the rolled-up *Book Review* and made her go lie down again. Later in the afternoon he told her to suck him while he did the crossword. When he got stuck on a word she would stop sucking him, if she knew the answer, and help him out. She sucked him for seven days while he came and grew soft and hard and came and slept and woke up hard, and at the end of the seven days he had finished the crossword and said, Now you can rub yourself against my leg until you come. Once again she rubbed herself against him and came almost immediately, and then licked his palm. He slapped her away, got up for a beer, and was gone forty days and forty nights. When he came back she had chewed up the couch cushions and gnawed on the coffee table and was lying on the floor with her tongue out. He expected her to be angry with him, but she only looked at him with large sorrowful eyes and begged to be fed. He gathered the newspapers spread on the floor where she had shit, and the potted plant where she had pissed, and after cleaning up and throwing out the cushions and turning the coffee table around so he couldn't see the gnawed leg, he ordered Chinese takeout and they ate together. When they were finished he cleared the empty cartons from the table and had her lie down on top of it. For the next thousand years he went to work and came home and each night they ate Chinese food; then she lay down on the coffee table and they watched TV for the rest of the evening. During the commercials he would lean down and suck on her breasts or put a finger up inside her, neither of them taking their eyes from the screen.

One night during a Toyota commercial, as he was moving his finger in and out of her, she came, closing her eyes during orgasm. When she opened them she was alone. The chain and collar were gone, and she was lying in a bed on top of a white sheet, naked, a ring of bright lights around the bed blinding her. Frightened, she curled into a ball in the middle of the bed, but after a few hours when nothing else happened she grew bored and curious, and sat up. She crawled to the edge of the bed to try and see who or what was on the other side of the lights. Out there it all looked black; she couldn't see anything so she stuck out one hand to feel for the floor. Cautiously she slid her hand farther and farther down, gripping the sheet with her other hand, then lying down on the bed to explore as far as the whole length of her arm, but still she couldn't feel anything solid. She imagined falling, into that black space where she would be swallowed up, hurtling through the darkness alone, and she drew up her hand and crawled back to the middle of the bed and lay there whimpering, waiting for the man to come back with the newspaper and the Chinese food, for she was suddenly very hungry, starving in fact she realized, and when he didn't arrive and didn't arrive after years and years and years she began to eat herself, starting with her hands and feet, and when she had devoured her legs and arms and cunt and belly and breasts, she started rocking back and forth on her head. Faster and faster she rocked, until at last she rolled off the edge of the bed, falling through the blackness and then the galaxies and finally the solar system, and when she got near earth she settled into orbit around it, waxing and waning and weeping.

# *trip*

He fucks a whore on a business trip to Bangkok. It doesn't mean anything. He goes to some bar, she takes him to a room. She undresses and lies down, opens her legs. Maybe she's not a woman, but a girl—thirteen, fourteen—from a small village. He's horny. He puts on the condom. She closes her eyes. Or maybe stares at the ceiling. He doesn't kiss her. He's probably a little drunk. Maybe more than that. He gets inside her. Maybe he sucks her tits. His hands are on either side of her breasts. Or she's turned over and he can't see anything but black hair, a small narrow back. Maybe his eyes are closed and he's only feeling the sensations in his body. He's in her cunt or her ass. She sucks him first or doesn't. There's music, or glasses clinking. Laughter or yelling. Maybe dim lights. Maybe he groans loudly, the way he always does when he comes. Maybe he doesn't come. He fucks her for a while and goes soft; he's too drunk. The girl starts giggling. Or just lies there. Or gets up to wash him off. She's older than he thought at first. Maybe younger. It's hot in the room. Maybe not a room but a curtained-off section of one, nothing in it but a bed and a towel. Maybe it's a cot. Maybe she's pretty. Or has pimples and bitten nails. He doesn't remember. He's back in America. He turns on some music, kisses me. He fucked a whore in Bangkok. I can't see her face. The room is dark. Maybe dim lights. Maybe not a room at all. He puts on the condom. He pushes inside. It doesn't mean anything.

# *reading*

I'm sick in bed with a high fever, and I'm reading. First I read in the newspaper about how dead bodies are used as crash test dummies in order to improve safety equipment in cars. Then I go to the bathroom and read *The New Yorker*, where I find out about Cambodian women who went blind after the Khmer Rouge soldiers came to their villages, tortured their neighbors, and swung their kids by the heels to smash their heads open on palm tree trunks. I go back to bed, my head aching, my body burning up, and read a short story about a guy who has an affair with his sister's Barbie. The sister mutilates Barbie—eats her feet off, gives her a partial mastectomy, sets her on fire. The mastectomy reminds me of something in the novel I started last night. A man who unloads bricks of cellophane from boxcars all day undresses a woman who turns out to have a huge, rock-hard lump in her breast. When I fell asleep, she was sitting in the Emergency Room and he was headed for the door, feeling sick. I finish the story about Barbie—it's the last one in the book—and masturbate for a while, then wonder what to read next. A fat black animal with yellow eyes is sitting at the end of the bed, staring at me like I'm insane, like it has to watch me every minute for fear of what I'll do next. I once read that cats hate to be stared at, that they take it as a sign of aggression. What you're supposed to do, meeting a strange cat for the first time, is look at it, blink and then cut your eyes quickly away, at the carpet or something. I try this on my cat, but she's suddenly disappeared. I look around the room. Books everywhere: piled on the nightstand, floating on the rumpled covers, lined up on brick-and-board shelves and on the windowsill. There's a stack of magazines in a yellow basket in the bathroom, magazines on the back of the toilet along with a book that has photos of Elvis impersonators and quotes from them about what it's like pretending to be Elvis. The next time I go to the bathroom I take some Tylenol and read in the introduction that Elvis is a bonafide American icon who lives in our collective unconscious, along with Davy Crockett, Johnny Appleseed, Wyatt Earp, and Pecos Bill. One of the impersonators, when he's not being Elvis, works as a hospital technician. I can't finish *The New Yorker* article yet; when I got to the part about the kids and the palm trees I put it down. I have to read it slowly, the way you can take belladonna in small doses so it won't kill you, just make you high and disoriented and give you hallucinations that make you think you're someplace you aren't. You might feel, for example, like you're at home in your own bed with a fever when you're really dying in a hospital, blind from everything you've tried not to see. You're convinced you're someone else, and when that person dies men in coveralls take the body and strap it into a car and send it slamming into a brick wall, then extract it from the crumpled wreckage and study it, making the world a little bit safer, the product a little bit better, the whole thing that much easier to bear.

# *in the box called pleasure*

My husband left me because he felt like he had no power. Now he has it; I call him up and beg him to come over and fuck me. I've just quit cigarettes, and all I can think about is how good it would feel to take a deep drag of smoke into my lungs. He pushes his cock down my throat until I gag on it, makes me keep it there until I have to relax; if I don't I'll choke. I relax. Everything is fine between us.

I have papers on my desk that read Dissolution of Marriage. I call and ask my husband for his Social Security number so I can fill them out, then I scream at him, then I don't do anything. I am having a crisis of self-esteem because I am ugly and stupid, with a bad memory to boot. I forget names, including my own, and most of what happened in books I read. *Madame Bovary*, for example. I remember that Emma kills herself, but not how. *Sentimental Education*: someone named Frédéric rides in a carriage and complains and is in love with a married woman. This is in the box called Flaubert. Also: origins of the modern novel. The Seine. Someone making love. A view of mist-covered pines from the apartment I rented one summer. End of box.

After I phone my husband he comes over and mashes me against the wall with his body. I love the feeling of being physically trapped. It's my worst fear, psychologically, why I ran from all my lovers before him. I realize I've lived by definitions; now there aren't any and it's impossible to function. Nature isn't friendly, but it exhibits a profound order. I think that if I could somehow stir myself into it as one more ingredient, I would know how to get through this. He's silent on the other end of the phone and I wonder what he's thinking, if he gives a shit if I live or die. The only way I can get over him is if I die.

I don't die.


I live in a mansion with ghosts. At night the former lady of the house floats, transparent, over the lawn, calling each of her children by name. Sometimes they answer. It's that or cats. A frieze over my fireplace shows a naked man in a chariot, a horse, cherubs, women in filmy robes. I don't touch anything for fear I'll break it. I can't remember how I got here, but it's pleasant enough. The floor shines, and there are windows all around, and a piece of furniture called a swooning couch. After a discrete knock, food appears on a tray outside my door; I never see the servants. Mostly I stay in my room, but sometimes I go down the wide red-carpeted staircase and into the drawing room, which is dark and filled with gloomy paintings of people I don't know in elaborate gold frames.

## kim addonizio

I masturbate constantly, imagining that my husband is ordering me to spread my legs. He slaps my thighs; if I try to close them he slaps them harder. He ties me to the brass bed, and I can't get up to answer the servants' knock. After he fucks me he throws a fire ladder out the window, climbs down it, and doesn't come back.

I call for help the first few days but nobody comes; nobody even knocks on the door anymore. After a few weeks I starve to death. I rise above my body, and it looks so pathetic I can't believe I didn't get rid of it sooner; my mouth is open, my eyes have a scummy film over them, there's shit and piss everywhere, not to mention blood because I got my period. I'm glad my ugly, filthy body can't drag me down any longer; now I'm light as a feather, I spin around near the ceiling feeling like I've just chain-smoked an entire pack of cigarettes. At first it's fun, but then I start to get bored with being dead and wonder what else there is to do. I decide to try masturbating, and guess what, it's great: when I come I fly into a million pieces, and it takes hours to collect myself from the corners of the room. I notice I can't go through walls, though, and that worries me. I don't want to be stuck here in this room with my body forever. It stinks, for one thing. A fly crawls over my cheek and into my mouth.

I'm lonely here, and I miss my husband. I write him a long letter, a letter full of questions about us. What is there between us, I ask him, besides our sex? Is there any point to staying married? What does that mean, anyway? We don't live together. We rarely see each other. I wear my wedding band on my right hand, if I wear it at all. His name is engraved on the inside so I won't forget it. Marriage is a) a capitalist institution for the subjugation of women and preservation of male power and authority, b) an anachronism, c) a way to get health insurance, d) a species of insect.

Dear, Darling, Sweetheart:
How I miss your hands on me, the smell of your skin, your tattoos, the harsh tobacco taste of your tongue. Though you should try not to smoke so much. I wish we could talk sometimes, instead of just fucking. You've become a total stranger to me except in bed, where I feel like we're the same person. I know it's the same for you. Marriage didn't kill our desire. Why can't we be friends? Don't you like me, just a little?
Love,
Your Wife

Every day I walk past the table in the hall where the servants leave the mail. There's nothing yet. Long-distance relationships suck. I wish there were someone here to fuck, but I'm too hung up on my husband to even consider it. Most men are lousy fucks anyway; that box is crammed full. Can't get it up, can't keep it up, won't eat pussy, comes in three seconds, holds me like I'm made of glass, can't find my clit, won't use a condom, fucks in total silence, expects me to do all the work, thinks of it as work, as proof of his power, as pure release: I have to come, there's a hole, I'd like to come in that but shit there's a person attached to it. My husband is an incredible fuck. I'm not sure what we do should even be called fucking. How can I give that up?

My husband left me to punish me; I wasn't behaving like A Wife. Fuck that. We didn't know each other very well. I'm starting to enjoy my freedom, even though my heart is a crushed useless lump of tissue that gurgles constantly like bad plumbing. I blame him for everything. Then I blame myself. Then I blame my father, my brothers, and God. It's impossible to have a relationship, nothing lasts anyway, there are no models, men go into the

woods and beat little drums and scream, gender is meaningless, or it's everything; I want a partner, I need to be
strong alone since we live and die alone anyway. I want
someone to love me. That's what everybody wants, right?
Besides being stupid, ugly, and amnesiac I am incapable
of seeing beyond my own selfish ego. Until I do, I'll never
get what I want.


Once we were happy.


Once he looked at me and I knew he loved and wanted
me and I wasn't scared he would stop.


Once there was a queen who was the most beautiful
woman in the land; everyone said so. Secretly, though,
she knew she was a disgusting, hideous creature who
had fooled everyone. Either that or she was totally insane. She didn't know which would be worse, to find
out she was really a monster or really a crazy nut, so she
ordered her subjects to remove all the mirrors from the
kingdom. Her husband the king humored her, but every
year on her birthday he tried to give her a mirror as a
present, figuring it was a phobia she would overcome in
time. Every year the queen refused the present and ordered the mirror taken out to the forest and smashed with
a hammer.

One year the king found such a gorgeously exquisite
mirror that the entire court urged the queen to accept it,
but it was the same old story: smash the shit out of it.
The woodsman whose job it was to do this took it out to
the forest, but he couldn't bring himself to ruin such a
beautiful object. He went deep into the forest, and there
he found a small house where he hid the mirror. He broke
a window in the house and brought the pieces back in a
leather bag, to prove to the queen that he had done her

bidding, and the queen put the bag in the bottom drawer of her dresser with all the other bags from previous years.

One afternoon when she was out jogging, the queen ran farther than she had ever run before, and came upon the little house hidden deep in the forest. Being extremely thirsty, she went inside to look for something to drink. As soon as she entered the house she saw the mirror, leaning against the wall under the broken window. She wanted to leave, but it was too late; as soon as she caught a glimpse of herself she stopped, transfixed, and couldn't look away.

I think all this has something to do with Lacan, whose theories I've forgotten.

Once we were fucking, I was on top, and between one thrust and the next I felt I didn't love him anymore. Suddenly I was just fucking a male body, not his body, and I felt a sense of freedom and power: now I could fuck anyone, do anything, create my own life. Then I was in love with him again, and I thought maybe I'd imagined it; can love go in and out like breath?

I've got to find a way to get out of here and get to town. In town there's a store: nail polish. Tampax. Liquor. Cigarettes. Lipstick. I don't have to wait here passively for something to happen. Do you think she saw a monster in the mirror? Makeup, in the seventies, meant slavery to imposed definitions of beauty; now it's assertive, self-adornment, a hip feminist statement.

I hate it that everything changes.

Themes so far: loss of power; loss of memory; self-hatred; definitions. A large crow lands on the lawn. In the box called pleasure:

144

I'm riding my bike around the streets of our neighborhood. My mom, who happens to be queen of the kingdom, has given me a letter to mail. I'm proud of being chosen to do this, especially since my mom never speaks to me; she spends most of her time shut up in her room, she's beautiful but crazy as a loon. But this morning she called me in, handed me a letter. Her stunning black hair was loose around her shoulders. She used to jog and work out and play tennis, but now she just lies around watching TV all day, and she's starting to get fat. I don't think she realizes this because there aren't any mirrors in the house; I have to go over to friends' houses to see what I look like. I'm blonde; I don't look a thing like my mother, but I'm cute as hell. I'm six years old and I want to be on TV. My name is Buffie. I adore my mother. When she gives me the letter I feel warm and happy; she hands it to me and kisses me on my forehead.

"Don't tell your brothers," she whispers. "Or your father, either. This will be our little secret. All right, darling?"

When she calls me "darling" I think I'll pass out from being so thrilled. I tuck the letter into a pocket of my dress. She turns back to "One Life to Live," and I go out of her room and down the stairs.

On the second floor I run into one of my seven brothers.

"C'mere, Buffie," he says. "I've got something in my room for you."

My seven brothers are all older than I am. They take me for pizza and ice cream, or ignore me; sometimes they protect me from our violent father, the king, and sometimes they tie me up and torment me.

"What've you got?" I say, suspicious. "I have to go do something for mom."

"It will only take a sec," my brother says.

I follow him into his room. My brother's room is filled with rats: cages and cages of them, sleeping in wood chips or running on treadmills or staring out at me, their tiny hands clawing at the wire mesh. They give me the creeps, like my brother. I don't trust him.

"Sit down there," my brother says, pointing to his bed. He has a can of Pam—spray-on cooking oil—in his right hand. He takes a baggie, sprays the Pam into the baggie, and holds it over my nose and mouth.

"Breathe, Buffie," my brother says.

I take a breath. Immediately my ears start ringing, the room recedes, I know I'm still in it, but I'm miles away; I can't find my body. I try to lift my hand, fall backwards on the bed; it takes hours to fall, I keep expecting to feel the bed but don't. I can hear my brother laughing somewhere. Then there's something hot between my legs and I feel like I have to pee, or maybe I am peeing; it's sticky, my underwear is wet; I try to move, but I'm trapped under something I can't see. I'm blind. I start to scream; I open my mouth and something cold rushes into my lungs, and I feel fantastic, I'm a big balloon, I start to giggle imagining myself as a balloon in a dress, my skin stretched tight over my enormous face I'm laughing so hard now I ache, more cold air filling me up I'm rocking back and forth in a rowboat in the middle of an ocean, rats are swimming by, their hairless tails whipping the water. The boat goes under.

I'm in my brother's room again. My head aches, I'm lying on his bed with my legs twisted open and my underwear off. He's standing over at the wall of cages, his back to me. He takes out a rat and brings it over to the bed.

"Ugh," I say. "Get it away from me." He knows I hate his rats.

"You'd better run," he says, smiling. He makes like he's going to toss the rat at me, but doesn't. I start crying. It hurts between my legs now. I jump up from his bed and run out, leaving my underwear.

I run downstairs to the garage and get on my bicycle. It's a pink five-speed Schwinn with streamers on the handles. As I ride, I feel more wetness come out of me.

I press my crotch against the bike seat, rub it back and forth.

At the mailbox on the corner I jump off my bike, then throw myself onto the grass. I lie on my stomach and put my fist under my cunt, between it and the ground, and grind against it. Cars drive by. I can't stop; I hope nobody pulls over. Finally I come. I've never masturbated before this. I don't understand what's just happened.

I remember my mother's letter and find it in my pocket, all wrinkled and creased. I smooth it as well as I can, then open the mailbox and drop the letter into its mouth.


Dear Woodsman:

I hate my husband, the king. Unless you become my lover I'm going to kill myself. I can't divorce him because I'm terrified to live on my own, without money. If I could look forward to seeing you each week, death wouldn't exert such a powerful pull. I can't live for my children; they're on their own. Meet me at the house in the woods, and bring condoms.

Your Queen


Letters are a woman's form. And diaries. The domestic isn't historical; in most of history women don't exist. The self is constituted in memory, so I don't have a self, just a few ideas for one. I sit for hours in the room that used to be my mother's, looking out at the lawn and the enormous fountain; it's the size of an Olympic swimming pool. I'm dying for a cigarette. I drink too much coffee, chew gum, bite my fingernails; I'm not going to make it. I pull Dante's box out of the closet. Open it a crack, flames and shit and vomit spill out; I've only read the *Inferno*. My mom's in there. The Geryon flies past my window, or maybe it's an eagle; I should get a bird book. I wonder why birds sing, anyway. Is it necessary for their survival?

There's one here that drives me crazy every morning, waking me at dawn. I'd like to sleep in, just once. All night it's ghosts, and then this fucking bird.


Dear Mom,
I don't know what the mail service is like down there, but I hope you get this in time for your birthday. Even though you were a lousy mother I loved you; I couldn't help it. I was only ten when you died. Why did you leave me? Why didn't you protect me from my brothers, those shits? My childhood was one long molestation. It's all your fault. How am I supposed to get past this and stop being a victim? Happy Birthday. I'm sorry there's no present but you were always so hard to buy for.
Love,
Buffie
p.s. Would you please stop calling my brothers' names every night? They are all doing fine. They have wives and ex-wives and girlfriends and kids and cocaine habits and big-screen TV's. You're the one that's dead.


I'm so depressed. I try to live as though life has meaning; I know it doesn't mean anything. You get old and sexually undesirable and then you die, or you kill yourself before that. Before my husband left me I felt loved, attractive, sexy: he grabs me by my cunt in the kitchen, leads me to the hall and fucks me on the floor, we're two animals; I love that he never thinks during sex or at least never seems to; I love being the instrument of his pleasure; I love the tiny space on his left eyelid—I think it's his left—where a lash is missing. I can't remember now. I've been abandoned. Or I set things up so he would abandon me; I didn't love him enough, my ex-lovers came out of the woodwork to have lunch and flirt, my husband was jealous, I didn't reassure him. Now I'm suffering.

In that box:

A six-year old boy on his way to school in LA gets caught in the crossfire between two gangs and dies. A man with a Serbian mother and Croatian father gets drafted into both armies, runs away to America; in America he drives a taxi in New York City in summer, a lower circle of hell. In the Wood of Suicides my mother moans. A woman answers an ad for a maid, goes to the door; it's a Hell's Angels house, they pull her inside and rape her, later she escapes out a window and goes home to her alcoholic mother. She's seventeen when all this happens, then finds out she's pregnant and gets an abortion, but it turns out she's carrying twins and the doctor has only aborted one. That night at home she's feverish, delirious, the second fetus comes out, she's hallucinating, passing out; she wakes up, blood all over the sheets. Before this her father fucked her for years; she finally told her mother, who had her committed. She's my best friend.

It is, after all, the love of women that sustains me.

Another friend says, "Do you feel that sex saved your life?" She means boys. Actually I think art saved my life at the time it needed saving, when I was doing too much heroin and fucking junkies and living in roach-filled apartments with gunshots in the street every night and the guy upstairs beating the shit out of his girlfriend. Now art isn't enough; I have that, and friends who love me— they write me letters, even if my husband doesn't—and I'm miserable.

One day I'm whining about my life and a girlfriend looks at me and says, "Well, Buffie, the important thing is to feel bad." She's right; I'm complaining about nothing, I should be grateful.

I'm still miserable.

There's a knock on the door. It's my husband, finally; he's come all this way to see me, he says he's sorry for everything and it doesn't matter what happened between us, whatever it was—who knows what's true or real anyway—he says, "I feel the pain and love and desire in your words to me and you're right, darling, sometimes it seems so perfectly simple and natural and right between us, even out of bed on occasion," he pushes me down on the bed, begins to rip my clothes off, *rip* my troubles are over *rip* this is a work of fiction and any resemblance to actual persons can't be helped, *rip rip* my underwear flies across the room, a bird goes up to heaven in a rush of wings and it starts raining, sheets of rain over the lawn and fountain, the roof of the house, the windows are streaming, *rip, rip, rip,* I can't stop remembering love.

# *about the author*

Kim Addonizio is the author of two books of poetry from BOA Editions: *The Philosopher's Club* and *Jimmy & Rita*. Her collection *Tell Me* is due from BOA in 2000. *The Poet's Companion: A Guide to the Pleasures of Writing Poetry*, co-authored with Dorianne Laux, was published by W.W. Norton. Addonizio's awards include two fellowships from the National Endowment for the Arts and a Pushcart Prize. She lives in San Francisco with her daughter, Aya.